addicted
TO
lust

A YAKUZA PATH ROMANCE

AMY TASUKADA

CONTENTS

ISBN ebook: 978-1-948361-28-6
ISBN Paper: 978-1-948361-29-3

Cover Design: Natasha Snow
Outline Critique: M.S. Wordsmith
Line Editing: Susie Selva
Copy Editing: Lyss Em
Interior Format: Rene Folsom

SYNOPSIS

Can a night of passion lead to a happily ever after?

Yakuza captain Hayato's life is a mess. His boyfriend broke up with him, changed the locks, and kept all his stuff. He can't crash at his brother's because his girlfriend is moving in. And just when Hayato thinks things can't get worse, he *accidentally* gets blackout drunk and wakes up in the arms of a clingy underling.

Masuo believes he and his boss made a deep connection, but when he's blown off the next morning, he feels lied to. Assigned to run a failing pachinko parlor, Masuo is determined to turn it around to prove himself to everyone...especially his sexy superior.

When Hayato realizes he's falling for the young parlor manager, he is more than ready for fun. But as Hayato's tragic past comes back to haunt him, Masuo wonders if he's ready to carry all Hayato's baggage.

Can the unlikely pair learn to accept each other and

find their way to happiness even while new challenges arise, or is their love destined to fall like balls through a pachinko machine?

ACKNOWLEDGMENTS

Thank you to my family, without whose support this book would not be possible. To Nell Iris, who is not only the queen of fluffy romance books but also a dear friend. Ash and Addison, thank you too for your comments and help. Leigh Hart, thanks for being my go-to plague buddy and your wonderful plotting ideas.

Finally, you. Thank you for giving my book a try.

J anuary sucked. Hayato always started it with a New Year's hangover. Then came the anniversary of the worst day of his life. And that wasn't including the cold. At least the snow was pretty sometimes, but January storms usually skipped the happily-ever-after fluffy snow and went straight to freezing rain of doom. No matter how many layers Hayato wore, he always froze his balls off. The whole month should be tossed out like a used condom in a love hotel's trash.

If he stayed in bed, he could pretend the calendar had never turned. He could go back to sweet December when nothing bad ever happened and the world was a blur of sales and romantic dinners. Or maybe he could stick with his current plan to spend the whole month of January drunk until the thirty-one days of hell passed and February dawned, if not warmer, at least a little brighter.

He hugged his pillow closer, then gagged, his sinuses assaulted by the stench of sweat and cum. Like the hangover wasn't bad enough. Only January 1 and already the month had lived up to its reputation as the one of suffering and hatred.

Hayato threw the pillow off the bed and rolled onto his back. Furry pink walls shocked any remaining sleep out of his system. The matching sheets and heart-shaped tufted headboard confirmed it. He'd spent the night at a love hotel. No big deal. No one wanted to spend New Year's alone. The sound of rushing water in the bathroom signaled Hayato needed to leave before things got complicated.

He clicked on the lights, bathing the room in a purple glow, which helped with the hangover but not in the get-dressed-and-scram department. His clothes were strewn about the hotel room like glitter at a drag show. His white lace shirt glowed in the dark night, but everything else might as well have been a black blob leading into the netherworld.

He reached under the bed. The familiar worn leather of his favorite pants made for one victory. He pulled them out, expecting to find his underwear inside, but they weren't. Hayato ran his fingers through his hair, the day-old hair spray knotting together what had once been delicate waves fashioned into his brown locks. His amethyst ring caught and ripped out a few strands. Hayato gagged at the sticky knot, hoping it was hair spray and not something else. He twisted the ball of hair and dumped it into the trash on top of three soiled condoms. Damn. Whoever he'd slept with must've been good. Too bad Hayato couldn't remember.

He crawled around the room and gathered the rest of his clothes.

Scarf, check.

Coat, check.

Super adorable gray cardigan with rainbow buttons, check.

But no underwear. Well, not *his* underwear. He'd found a pair of boring plaid boxers. Definitely not his and definitely changed his opinion about last night's partner. Hayato mentally demoted his partner from Mr. Impressive down to Mr. Good at Sex but No Taste.

Had Hayato even worn underwear to the Fushimi ward's New Year's party? The whole evening was too fogged over with alcohol for him to remember. The water in the bathroom stopped. Screw the underwear. He preferred going commando anyway. He bent down to kick on the first leg of his pants.

The door opened.

Hayato's jaw dropped. Mr. Good at Sex but No Taste switched back to Mr. Impressive.

No. That name wasn't enough for the man before him.

Maybe Mr. Hung Like a Horse, or Mr. Screw Me into Next Month, or Mr.—

"The shower's free if you want to go next," the man said, his voice husky and sweet like bourbon stirred with a cinnamon stick.

He grabbed a towel and wrapped it teasingly low around his hips. His dark nipples and the way he bit at his lip ring after speaking made Hayato lose all will to attempt to pull up his pants.

"Unless you have something else in mind." He looked down at the forgotten leather in Hayato's hands and grinned like only a cocky early twentysomething who'd spent the last night making a man ten years older writhe and moan all night could.

"Nah." Hayato slid the leather up his legs. "I'm heading out."

"Can I have your number?"

Hayato laughed.

"What's so funny?"

"It's cute. You asking and all." Hayato zipped up his fly.

Mr. Bourbon and Cinnamon's sandy-brown eyes narrowed, then he leaned against the wall and crossed his arms. The man seemed to enjoy the gym, but it would take more than a little bicep muscle to distract Hayato. At least without a few drinks in him first.

Hayato slid his arms through his sleeves and buttoned up his shirt. "I'm sure we had a nice time last night, but I have a boyfriend."

"What? You told me you weren't seeing anyone." His mouth dropped open. His pouty lips probably looked great around a cock.

"I'm not."

"But you just said you have a boyfriend."

Hayato rolled his eyes. "We're getting back together today."

Mr. Bourbon and Cinnamon shook his head, dripping dark strands of hair framing his youthful face. "That doesn't make any sense. You were the one who suggested we go to a love hotel in the first place."

Hayato sighed, took a tube of Temptation Rose lip gloss out of his pocket, and dabbed it on his lips. Was this boy going to make Hayato explain his whole life?

"See, Jiro and I got into a fight on Christmas," Hayato said.

"And you broke up?"

"Sure." Going slow seemed to work for the kid, so Hayato stuck with it. "Jiro overreacted because he's a high-strung salaryman who worries the world is ending when the Nikkei goes down twenty points. But it's been almost a week. He's cooled off by now, and we're going to get back together. Today. I need to talk to him first. So you see, that's why I can't give you my number. It would make things awkward."

"It sounds like you and Jiro are over. Forget about your ex and give me a chance."

He and Jiro weren't over. Hayato wrapped his scarf around his neck, tying the ends into a loose knot.

"I wish you a good New Year." Hayato kept his language formal and stiff.

The boy took a step forward. "We had great chemistry. We'd be awesome together."

Begging outside the bedroom was the biggest turnoff.

Hayato couldn't listen anymore. He grabbed his socks, stuffed his feet into his shoes, and left. How could someone be so clingy after a single night?

2

H ayato couldn't reunite with his love with last night's hair spray, or other mysterious substances, in his hair, so he snuck into his brother's tiny studio apartment, where he'd been crashing for most of the week. Subaru worked nights and would sleep well into the afternoon. He'd never hear the shower run.

Hayato needed to look his best, so he curled his hair into styled wisps pushed to the right, covering an eye. Jiro had once confessed Hayato's alluring one-eyed look was a major turn-on, and today, Hayato wasn't taking any chances. He smacked on a fresh layer of lip gloss, but nothing could hide his work suit. Hopefully it wouldn't upset Jiro, but he hadn't left Hayato much choice.

He exited the apartment and got on the train. It would only take a few stops, then he'd be home. He couldn't wait to return to Jiro and get that sweet, sweet make-up sex. Especially since Jiro had a lot of making up to do.

They were going to screw in the shower, and in the

kitchen, and on the balcony. And if Jiro complained about how the neighbors might see or how unhygienic screwing in the kitchen was, well, maybe Hayato would walk out on him. Then he'd see how it felt to have the door slammed in his face.

A cold breeze cut through Hayato's power fantasy. Even joking about walking out made his heart pound louder than rain on a metal roof. Jiro was the missing piece in Hayato's life, what made him whole. They simply fit. The week without Jiro had left Hayato broken and alone.

His phone chimed, and a small gasp escaped his lips. The air fogged around him. It had to be Jiro, finally replying with how excited he was to have Hayato home. How the ten-minute walk from the train station was too long and Hayato needed to run!

Hayato pulled out his phone and checked the screen. His smile faded. His glossed lips pressed into a thin line.

Jiro hadn't texted at all. Not now and not in the last five days. All Hayato's voicemails had also gone unreturned.

Hayato shook his head and replied to the pachinko parlor manager's *Happy New Year* message with a smiley face and goat emoji. Then Hayato texted the dozen other managers he directed with a similar New Year's message of joy, even if darkness had clouded his heart.

He shoved the phone back into his pocket and warmed his hands with his breath. They lived way too far from the train station. With each step, he rehearsed what he'd say to Jiro. Hayato would forgive him, sure, but Jiro would have to promise not to flip out over something small again.

The apartment doorman opened the door. Hayato smiled and wished him a happy New Year, ignoring that the man mentioned not seeing him the past few days.

Hayato stepped into an elevator and made his way to the eleventh floor. The boring burgundy carpet and fake plants had never looked so welcoming. Even the gaudy golden baroque wallpaper sung.

He came to his door and stuck his key into the lock, but it wouldn't turn. Hayato narrowed his eyes and tried again.

Nothing.

A sharp pain struck his heart. He and Jiro were meant for each other. They couldn't continue their life together if Hayato couldn't open the door.

"The overreacting bastard changed the locks," he grumbled.

The elevator dinged, and Hayato glanced over. Jiro strolled out, boxes of New Year's food stacked so high in his arms he couldn't see over them. Hayato had had to practically beg Jiro to pick what dishes he wanted before the store sold out, and here Jiro was, strolling down the hall, ready to eat both servings like it had all been his idea.

Hayato doubled back, but Jiro must've seen him because he darted into the elevator. He balanced the boxed food in one hand while furiously clicking a button with the other. Hayato stuck his hand between the closing doors.

Jiro said nothing, and not a single bone in his smug body turned.

Hayato cleared his throat and put a hand to his chest.

"I wanted to say I forgive you. Now give me the key to our apartment."

Jiro laughed, then peeked his head out from behind the boxes. His cold eyes and his short low-level-management haircut made him appear even more frigid. Hayato wasn't one of his employees. Jiro couldn't fire him because he said something Jiro didn't like.

"It's been almost a week. You've had time to cool off." Hayato hated the pleading tone in his voice.

"I told you. We're over."

Hayato winced and clutched his stomach. Jiro's words cut like a blade. Pain welled in Hayato's chest and throat. It couldn't be the end.

"You know, at first I thought you were joking, like you were trying to get me to do one of your crazy BDSM role-playing things again. I mean, come on, what yakuza paints his toes like a magical girl every Sunday?"

"It shouldn't ma—"

"But then I remembered your brother. Even thinking about him gives me chills. He's a yakuza, isn't he? No, don't tell me. I don't want to know. I don't want to get any more involved."

"Subaru has nothing to do with us."

"We had this argument on Christmas. I'm not going to change my mind," Jiro said.

"We've been together for two years."

"If the company ever found out I was dating a yakuza, my career would be over. I can't take a chance. Not when there's an upper-middle-management position opening up."

The reunion of his dream had been so much sweeter. Instead, Hayato's anger burned quickly, leaving his limbs heavy and dulling all his senses. Heat flushed through his body like a flame singeing timber.

"Did it all mean nothing to you?" Hayato asked. "I tell you the truth and then you throw me out like garbage. You didn't answer my calls and now you change the locks. Did you even stop to think about me? About us?"

Jiro shook his head. "It's over, Hayato. It's been over for a while. We've been going through the motions for months. Now I'm going to pretend it never happened, and you should too."

"What?"

The elevator lurched to a stop.

"If you'll excuse me, sir. I will be on my way," Jiro said.

The doors opened, and Jiro escaped as someone walked in. Hayato stuck out his head. Jiro strolled to the stairs on the other side of the hall.

"What about my stuff!" he yelled.

Jiro didn't even look back.

The doors shut, and Hayato rode the elevator down to the lobby.

Jiro's callous words had scorched Hayato's heart until it scarred, and he felt nothing. Two years down the drain. Their life together, the future they'd planned.

Hayato's phone rang, and he slowly took it out of his pocket. Endo's name flashed on the screen. Finding a quiet place in the lobby proved difficult with the bustle of families, but Hayato found an abandoned chair near the back exit.

"Ward Leader Endo," Hayato answered, hoping his voice didn't shake as much as his heart ached. The last thing he needed was his boss thinking he couldn't control his emotions.

"I got some new work for you today." Her firm tone left no room for argument. Not that Hayato would ever dare.

"I understand. Whatever you need, I won't fail you."

"Masuo graduated to officer. You probably met him at the party last night."

Everyone from the ward had come to the party. With so many people, Hayato would've had a hard time remembering everyone even without the haze of alcohol.

"He's the idiot who broke the Mayumaro figurine," she added. "So it's your job to show the klutz how to run things. I'm sticking him in the parlor underneath the club. As long as he doesn't do anything stupid, it should be fine. We need to get it open and making profits."

"Got it," Hayato said. "I'll see he's set up right."

"You're in charge of him now, so make sure he's not a fuckup. He'll meet you there at three."

"I won't let you down. By the way, the party location was per—"

She hung up.

Hayato twisted the ring on his finger. Three months of service to the Fushimi ward and she still treated him like an outsider.

3

Masuo folded the crisp black tie into a half-Windsor knot, then tugged down his shirt sleeves, loving the flash of white against his dark blazer. Did the suit make the man? Masuo wasn't sure, but the bespoke design from Ota Clothiers sure made him feel like a full-fledged yakuza.

When Endo had given him his job placement that afternoon, he'd been a little shocked but not as much as when she'd told him who his boss was going to be. A colorful gift bag seemed like the perfect way to return his new boss's forgotten underwear.

Masuo grabbed the gift bag and headed out. He locked his apartment and caught his next-door neighbor, Kira, leaving too. She was a pretty woman with long hair and a smile that always put Masuo at ease. Her young son and daughter came out dressed in big puffy black coats. They looked like shiny New Year's black beans. Masuo watched them a few nights each week when Kira worked the late shift.

"Look, Mama! It's Masuo." Sakura, Kira's four-year-old daughter, tugged on her mother's coat and pointed.

Masuo waved. "You heading to the shrine?"

Six-year-old Daichi grabbed onto Masuo's hand. "You should come with us."

Masuo squatted down to the kid's level. "Sorry, I won't be able to join you."

Daichi frowned, and it twisted Masuo's heart like all the times he'd watched his parents leave for work. Masuo took some money out of his pocket and handed the coins to Daichi.

"Since you're going to the shrine, can you get me a good-luck charm?" Masuo asked.

"I'll get you the luckiest one."

"Daichi, you're the best!"

"Congratulations on the promotion," Kira said.

"Thanks." Masuo stood. "I'm excited to finally be able to prove myself."

"Do you know when you get your schedule?"

"I'm not sure yet. Once I know, I'll text you." Masuo hoped his smile came off as sincere as he felt. He knew it would be difficult for Kira. "The local childcare office hasn't gotten back to you?"

"Not yet."

"The government is ridiculous when it comes to simple things like that. So much bureaucracy to even set up things like a day care." Masuo shook his head and sighed. "You have a nice time. I gotta get going. See you soon."

Masuo waved goodbye to the trio, then headed off. The train station had never looked brighter, and he'd never felt more like a yakuza. Even the people around him took notice, moving aside as he walked.

The parlor was a fifteen-minute walk from the station. Only a few people dotted the charming brick street. Maybe at night it picked up, since the clubs attracted people.

Masuo stopped in front of his parlor. A dirty mural of *Lupin the Third* greeted him. The windows were covered in the thick grime of neglect. If the previous manager had made the effort to make even a closed parlor look attractive with a timeless character like Lupin, then the insides had to have the same care. Masuo took out his handkerchief and tried to clean a window.

"What are you doing here?" Hayato asked, voice low and daring like a true yakuza boss who was ready to bash some skulls.

No one should be allowed to look so effortlessly gorgeous. His suit, cut close to his body, showed his lean lines of muscle. Yesterday, Hayato had taken Masuo's heart, but today, Hayato stole Masuo's breath. It took everything for him to stop mentally undressing his new boss.

"Well?" Hayato crossed his arms.

"You're giving me the key." Masuo clutched the gift bag and stood a little straighter, putting him taller than Hayato.

"You're Masuo?" Hayato's eyes went wide, and he rubbed his temples. "I can't believe I slept with the idiot who broke the Mayumaro figurine."

The figurine had haunted Masuo since his first day at the Fushimi ward. He'd dropped the prized forty-five-year-old figure of the mascot of Kyoto while cleaning. The creepy silkworm with no mouth had shattered into so many pieces it had taken Masuo all day to glue it back together.

"I'm not an idiot," Masuo said. "Other recruits who graduated before me were placed as workers at the other parlors. Ward Leader Endo put me in charge of this one all by myself."

"Oh, honey, you're like a cute little lamb. This place is a hole-in-the-wall. The profits are a drop in the ocean compared to the other parlors. Endo put you here because no one else was available, since so many of us were killed after the Double Moon attacks."

Masuo's stomach churned, but he swallowed back the ball of anger crawling up his throat and opened his mouth to speak.

"What's that?" Hayato pointed to the bright bag. "Is it a gift to butter me up?"

Hayato needed to be taken down a peg, and what Masuo had inside the bag would do nicely for that purpose. Masuo held it out, and Hayato reached inside. He pulled out a pair of banana-printed micro briefs.

But Hayato's face didn't grow red. He showed no sign of embarrassment at all.

Masuo sucked in his lip ring. "If you left these at the hotel, it must mean you don't wear underwear often. Are you wearing any now?"

Hayato grinned. "Don't you wish you could find out."

The cheeky comeback smacked Masuo, but he wasn't sure if it was a slap in the face or a playful tap on the ass.

"We need to get down to business," Hayato said. "First, take the lip ring out."

"You liked it last night."

Hayato crossed his arms. "Look, I can't even remember last night, so it must not have been that good. You can take that I-made-you-come smirk off your face and do what you're told."

"You don't remember? I was shit-faced drunk too, but you said it was the best sex you'd had in years."

"I don't doubt it. Jiro thought screwing on the sofa was spicing things up."

It all clicked for Masuo.

"You cheated on him with me to make your ex jealous so he'd get back with you."

"I'm not a cheater."

Hayato opened the gate of the parlor and eyed Masuo until he took out his lip ring. He slipped the ring into his pocket, and they entered the parlor.

Dust covered the dozens of machines arranged in two long rows. The seats were ripped, and dark stains peppered the carpeted floor. It hadn't been updated since the seventies.

"Is this place even structurally sound?" Masuo asked. "It can't be up to date with all the earthquake codes."

Hayato shrugged. "Hasn't fallen down yet."

With the dance club above, Masuo could only see the cracks in the ceiling getting worse.

Hayato leaned against the prize counter.

"Since you're technically the manager, you can set your hours, but to make the profit Endo expects from this place, the last guy had it open six days a week from ten to ten. If you don't make a profit, you can kiss that day off goodbye."

"I know what I'm doing."

"You've run a parlor before?"

17

"No."

"I make my point." Hayato twirled his hand. "If you somehow develop a magical way to make this place rain money, maybe Endo will throw you the next graduating recruit to help you."

Masuo wrote all the details in a well-worn pocket notebook. He didn't want to miss anything.

"I'll come by every day at about six to collect the money and return the plastic prize coins," Hayato said.

The prize coins allowed the parlors to circumnavigate the antigambling laws. People bought balls to play on the pachinko machines. They'd win or lose more depending on their skill. The winnings were counted, and patrons were allowed to pick from a collection of prizes. If they wanted actual money, they'd pick worthless gold plastic coins, then they'd go around the corner to a little window store and exchange the plastic coins for cash. The parlor and the exchange were technically different businesses, thus making it legal.

"Do you understand everything, or do I need to repeat myself?" The tone of Hayato's voice squeezed Masuo's heart.

The Hayato before him was so different from the one Masuo had met at the New Year's party. *That* Hayato had talked with everyone and made sure they enjoyed the festivities. *That* Hayato had spent hours beside with Masuo, who had been huddled by the exit. *That* Hayato had held Masuo's hand all night no matter how he'd twisted and turned when he'd slept.

Masuo flexed his hand. He'd thought they'd had a deep connection, but it was a lie. Hayato was some one-night-stands-mean-nothing guy who thought Masuo was an idiot like everyone else. Masuo would show him.

"I got it," Masuo said.

"Good. Come into the office."

He followed Hayato through the door behind the prize counter to a tiny vomit-green-colored room. An ashtray filled with cigarettes sat on the corner of a desk along with a family photo. Masuo gulped, and a sinking feeling set in. He'd been a new enough recruit that he hadn't seen any action during the war with the Double Moon, but it didn't mean others hadn't been affected.

"This is the combination for the safe." Hayato pointed to a closet. "The safe is in there. Go practice opening it."

"I can open up a safe."

"I don't want to come here tomorrow and find out you couldn't lock up any money, so do as you're ordered."

Masuo bit his lip but didn't say anything. Humiliation coursed through his veins, but he opened the closet and then entered the code to the little safe in the corner. Hayato was a bastard.

"There, it's open," Masuo said.

Hayato looked inside. "Good. I'll be back tomorrow when the parlor officially opens."

Hayato headed out of the office.

"Wait!" Masuo called.

Hayato turned back. "You're still not getting my number."

"That's the last thing on my mind now. Don't I get any money to help update the place?"

Hayato rolled his eyes but pulled out his wallet. He counted out five crisp ten-thousand-yen notes. "There. That should be enough."

"To paint or replace the carpet, maybe. But these machines are ancient. No one will want to play one."

"Don't you know what you're doing?" Hayato repeated Masuo's words back at him.

Hayato walked out, and Masuo couldn't help but allow his gaze to linger on his perfect ass. Masuo cursed himself. Hayato might look the same, but he wasn't. As far as Masuo was concerned, he'd just met the real Hayato, and there was no way Masuo wanted to rekindle the feelings they'd shared the previous night.

4

Masuo rubbed the damp washcloth over the pachinko machine. The car-racing theme might've been popular in the eighties, but no one would want to play it today. Not when all the other parlors in the ward had machines with LCD screens playing video segments of anime characters shoving their boobs in the players' faces.

It took three hours to take half the machines from grime-covered dust collectors to ready for action, but no matter how much Masuo scrubbed, the parlor would never turn into his dream to show Endo he was competent.

The floors, the dull-colored walls—Masuo didn't know where to start. Not that he had the money to do anything worthwhile.

Masuo sighed and banged his head against the clunker of a pachinko machine in front of him.

"Hey!" Arashi called from the front of the parlor.

Arashi had been friends with Masuo since the broken-figurine incident. Arashi stood taller than Masuo, and with his long hair and relaxed attitude, he belonged at the beach or in some pop-idol group as the easygoing one. Arashi had graduated the month before and had been placed at the ward's biggest parlor—three floors filled with everything from pachinko machines to slots. Even though Arashi was a low-level worker, he had more experience than Masuo.

"Manager of this whole place by yourself. Congrats, man. It's so awesome." Arashi cradled a potted orchid in one arm and held up his other hand for a high-five.

"This parlor is a shithole."

"But it's your shithole." Arashi held his hand a little closer and wiggled his fingers. "Come on, don't leave me hanging."

Masuo reluctantly completed his half of the high-five. Arashi held their hands up like they'd won a relay race. He cheered too much for his own good, but he succeeded in making Masuo smile.

"For you." He handed Masuo the plant.

"Thanks."

"It's not that bad." Arashi stepped inside. "You're going for a late Showa-era look, right?"

"This place was operational last year. I don't understand how he got enough people to come to make a profit." Masuo placed the plant on top of one of the barstool seats, ignoring the large rip down the side.

Arashi shrugged. "Maybe people came for the nostalgic feeling."

"Nostalgia only gets you so far. They'll come here once, feel nostalgic, and won't need to come back."

"You'll figure it out."

Masuo sighed. He grabbed the washcloth and rubbed against a particularly grimy spot on a nearby machine.

"Have you been cleaning with the same mad look on your face the whole day?" Arashi asked.

"I'm not incompetent."

"I didn't say you were." Arashi folded his arms. "Did someone bring up the Mayumaro statue again?"

"Endo put me here to fail, I know it, but I'm going to turn it around. I'm going to make it more profitable than it ever was. I'll show her and Hayato."

"If anyone can do it, you can. No one thought you could piece the Mayumaro statue back together, but you had the silkworm in one piece that very night." Arashi's words struck Masuo's heart like a double jackpot.

Masuo squeezed the damp washcloth in his hand, and water dripped out along with his last droplet of doubt. His chest puffed out, and he turned up his chin.

"Want to help me pull up the carpet?" Masuo asked.

"Why don't I help you finish a sake flask?" Arashi said. "Celebrating will help you figure out a plan."

"I need to finish scrubbing the rest of the machines."

Arashi grabbed another cloth. "If it gets us drunk sooner, I'll help."

Scrubbing took half the time with Arashi's help. His stories of the worst customers at his parlor were a mix of hilarious and gross, but they helped pass the time. More importantly they made Masuo forget how irritating Hayato was...almost.

With the last machine sparkling, they made their way to Masuo's favorite bar. A small sake bar that fit fewer people than a train car. The dark lighting immediately

23

relaxed his shoulders, and the soft jazz playing allowed time to slip away.

Arashi and Masuo slid into a well-worn booth and ordered some sake. Once the hot sake came, they filled each other's cups, and Arashi held his up.

"To Masuo becoming the best parlor manager in the ward," Arashi said.

Masuo laughed, and they clinked their glasses together and sipped. The hot alcohol was perfect against the chilly January weather.

Masuo pulled out his mini notebook. "I want to hear all the parlor management tips you have."

"You're not even going to ask me how the dating app is going?"

"How's the dating?"

"Horrible." Arashi pulled out his phone and poked around on it. "I found a girl I like. It says she enjoys horror films. Cool, right? So I message her and say I like them too and ask her what her favorite is, but no response."

Masuo shrugged. "Maybe she's busy. When did you message her?"

"Three days ago."

"Oh." Masuo took a sip of sake.

"That's all you're going to say?" Arashi faked being shocked.

"There're lots of other ladies out there for you."

"You got it easy. You can go out with anyone."

Masuo rolled his eyes. "Just because I'm bi doesn't mean I'm attracted to everyone."

"Speaking of which, why are you even asking me for

tips? You slept with the boss. Hayato would be the one with all the best suggestions. Ask him."

"He doesn't remember," Masuo mumbled and took another sip of sake.

"Huh?"

"I said Hayato doesn't remember last night."

Arashi laughed. "You must not be as good as you thought."

Masuo didn't say anything, but the way Hayato had moaned proved he'd had a good time. Arashi kept laughing, then refilled Masuo's drink and laughed some more.

Masuo rolled his eyes. "Hayato's an ass anyway."

"What? Hayato? No. He's super nice."

"No. He's an asshole."

Arashi shook his head. "You got it wrong. My first week, the night manager got super sick with the flu and left early. Hayato came and helped us all lock up. He even bought everyone snacks after."

"You're lying. No one makes it to captain as a yakuza being that nice."

"Well, somehow he did."

"He probably fucked someone."

Arashi laughed. "Who?"

"Father Murata."

They both laughed.

Arashi sipped his drink. "You know what Hayato is doing? I think he's being strict with you, since you're a manager and running the whole thing by yourself."

"Or maybe he's an asshole."

"Time will tell." Arashi sighed into his sake cup. "So you want parlor tips?"

"Yes. Tell me everything your manager told you."

Masuo would fill the pages of his notebook with every tip Arashi gave.

5

Hayato nuzzled his pillow, engulfed himself in his comforter cocoon, and ignored his brother coming home from work.

Subaru's job as a host-club manager meant he didn't get home until the unholy hour of four in the morning. Hayato couldn't muster up enough energy to say "welcome home," let alone explain why he hadn't returned home to Jiro.

Subaru's weight pressed onto the bed, and he mumbled something and wouldn't stop. Sure, Hayato was supposed to be gone, but they weren't just brothers. They were identical twins. Subaru would understand.

And Hayato would explain everything in the afternoon once Subaru slept off his scary manager mode and, hopefully, turned into the most understanding twin in the world.

Then a weight crashed into Hayato's cocoon and elbowed him in the gut. He narrowed his eyes and pulled back the covers. Luckily, Subaru hadn't decided to reenact their childhood roughhousing but instead was tongue deep in a kiss with his girlfriend, Fumiko.

"I think you're on my spleen," Hayato said.

Fumiko pulled away from the kiss and removed her arm from Hayato's gut. The streetlight illuminated her rounded features in a delicate glow. She'd styled her hair in the same wavy curls she wore during dance competitions. Wait. If she'd dressed for a Lindy Hop... Shit! It wasn't four in the morning but one. Subaru must've had the night off.

"This was your first New Year's date, wasn't it?" Hayato bit his lip. "Sorry for messing it up."

The first date of the year set the tone for the rest, and thanks to him, Subaru was destined to not get laid for the remaining 363 days.

Fumiko's smile was as sunny as her flower-printed dress, but Subaru gave Hayato *that* look. The look only a three-minutes-older brother who took his status way too seriously could give. Hayato's stomach flopped like a ball of mochi, and he looked away. Not texting Subaru a heads-up about staying a few extra days had been a mistake.

"Did Jiro's business trip get extended?" Fumiko asked.

A nervous laugh crept up Hayato's throat. "We...ah, kind of got into a big fight."

"Oh no, I'm sorry. He didn't dump you on New Year's, did he? What a jerk!" Fumiko held up a fist. "Want me to give him a good talking-to?"

Hayato's smile hurt. He didn't deserve all Fumiko's kindness, but it did help balance Subaru's glare of a thousand lectures.

"No worries," Hayato said. "I already gave him something to think about."

Sure, he gave Jiro a lot of stuff to think about, like how Hayato had picked out the most delicious New Year's food for them or what to do with all his clothes taking up their bedroom closet.

Subaru shook his head, his eyes speaking every word of his disappointment.

Fumiko slid off the bed and gave Subaru a peck on the cheek. "It's getting late, honey cake. I should probably get going."

They might've been twins, and Subaru even dyed his hair the same golden bronze as Hayato, but there the similarities ended.

Hayato liked men. Subaru liked women.

Hayato talked too much. Subaru listened.

Hayato looked like a skinny twink. Subaru looked like a gym rat. No one outside their boogie-woogie dance community knew all the muscles were for swinging Fumiko over his head. Not to mention, Subaru was the perfect beacon of generosity, kindness, and self-sacrifice. How had Hayato ended up as bad as he had with Mr. Perfect as an example?

Subaru escorted Fumiko to the door, and they whispered to each other before a final passionate goodbye kiss.

Once Fumiko left, Subaru disappeared into the bathroom, and the electronic hum of his toothbrush echoed in the small place. He came out a few minutes later, ready for bed.

"Sorry." Hayato's apology felt wholly inadequate.

"We'll talk in the morning." Subaru pulled the covers over his shoulders and turned his back toward Hayato.

Hayato hugged his pillow and pretended the cold shoulder didn't hurt. A bottle of wine and the knowledge that Subaru would be home in a few hours had been the only way he'd managed to fall asleep in the first place. He couldn't go to sleep knowing he'd pissed off Subaru enough to make him even quieter than usual. Especially in January.

How long Hayato lay there with his head buried in his pillow and thoughts swirling he wasn't sure, but at some point, Subaru's light snoring broke through the maelstrom. Centimeter by centimeter, Hayato squished closer until the mattress dipped and Subaru's warmth radiated around him.

Hayato wasn't alone. Subaru was there. Only then could Hayato quiet his monophobic thoughts and find sleep.

HAYATO STRETCHED OUT HIS ARM, but no one slept beside him. A shock burned through his cold fingers, jolting him awake. Any notion of returning to sleep disappeared.

Hayato looked around and found Subaru drinking a beer at the tiny table next to the wall. The decorative label on the bottle looked expensive. Hayato sure had to have fucked up to send Subaru for the good stuff.

Hayato clenched his fingers around the bedsheet. He'd have to confess all his failures sometime. He slipped off the covers and grabbed a gray robe. Unfortunately, the robe didn't feel like armor, and he spun the ring around his finger to center his thoughts.

Hayato moved to sit opposite his brother. "Sorry for messing up your evening with Fumiko. Did you guys have a fun date at least?"

"We got second at the New Year's Lindy Hop." Subaru pulled the beer away from his mouth so the words came clearly before taking another swig.

"That's awesome. Congratulations!"

Subaru's stoic expression didn't change.

Hayato rubbed the back of his neck. "It must've sucked having me cockblock you."

Subaru said nothing back, which only weighed down Hayato more.

"I lied about Jiro's business trip," Hayato said.

Subaru could beat Hayato down with a look, and the longer his brother's silence wore on, the more it ate at him.

"Jiro and I got into a fight on Christmas, and I figured by New Year's he would've cooled off, but he didn't, and now...and now..." Hayato's voice cracked, and tears leaked out with the truth.

Subaru's chair scraped across the wooden floor. He closed the distance between them in an instant and hugged Hayato. The brotherly hug warmed him but also pushed Hayato back to the day when their world had turned upside down. He clutched onto his brother. He'd always be there.

"I'm sorry you and Jiro didn't work out. I know you loved him," Subaru said.

A heaviness knocked against Hayato's stomach because his heart railed against the lie. Over the past year, he'd become indifferent in his relationship with Jiro. The energy and enthusiasm had been gone. Hayato had confessed to being a yakuza in hopes it would get their energy back. Too bad it had blown up in his face.

He hadn't fought hard to get Jiro back, specifically. He only wanted his committed company. Hayato wanted someone beside him. Even though they'd grown apart, having Jiro beside him would have been better than facing the month alone.

"It's just, you know, Mom's death and... her depression leading up to it." Hayato pulled back, dabbing his eyes with the sleeve of his robe. "Sorry."

"It's a hard month for me too." Subaru's lips pressed into a thin line. "Especially this year. We're the same age she was. Come May, we'll be older. How are children supposed to be older than their mother? It's not right, and if I think too hard, I get as upset as you are."

"I'm okay," Hayato lied, hoping that hearing the words might subconsciously trick him into believing them.

"Still, you should've told me about you and Jiro sooner—"

"I know. It was stupid. I thought I could fix it."

"Last night I asked Fumiko to move in with me. She said yes. Her lease is up next week."

Hayato's eyes widened. He swallowed the lump in his throat, but it was like a match to tinder in his stomach. Where was he going to live? Subaru's apartment barely fit one. Three would be impossible. Hayato would have to move out. Find his own place.

Live alone.

He'd never lived alone in his life. The closest he'd come was two years ago when Subaru and Fumiko had first started dating. Subaru had been too busy practicing jigs and swing steps to look at the clock. Hayato couldn't stand waiting, so he'd gone to the clubs. He'd met Jiro, and he'd been a lifesaver. His dependability had made up for his boring personality, and a month later, they'd moved in together.

"Congratulations." Hayato hoped he sounded sincere. "I'll be out of here by the time she moves in."

Subaru squeezed his brother's shoulder. "I can help you look for a place."

"I'll be fine," Hayato lied again and knew Subaru could tell with his stupid older-twin powers.

But Subaru played along, and why wouldn't he? He was looking forward to all the things society said he should want: marriage, kids, a cute little house, and a fluffy dog called Snuggles. But Subaru couldn't do any of those things with his brother tagging along. It didn't matter if being alone for more than half an hour gave Hayato heart palpitations.

"I know your monophobia gets bad sometimes," Subaru said, accidentally twisting the knife a little more.

Hayato laughed and waved his hand. "I got over that years ago." Another lie.

"If you change your mind, I understand."

Hayato wanted his brother to have a life with Fumiko. Fumiko would make a wonderful sister-in-law who could hold her own as a yakuza's wife. Their children would be adorable, and their dog would be so disgustingly cute they'd give it its own social media page. It would probably end up with more followers than most D-list celebrities. The only thing stopping Subaru from his future and true happiness was Hayato. He couldn't hold his brother back anymore. He needed to find some way to live by himself.

"I want my own place, so don't even think about asking me to change my mind." Hayato laughed. "You'll need to get busy cleaning up all those dildos and porn mags under the bed before Fumiko moves in."

"Those are yours." Subaru laughed, and Hayato already missed the rich, soulful sound.

"Jiro thought all that stuff was too kinky, and I wasn't about to throw it all away. Those things are expensive." Hayato took a few steps toward the bathroom, his heart pounding in his chest. "Don't worry, I'll be out of your hair in no time."

"She can get a place for a month if you can't find anything."

"Nope. No, no, no. I'll find something. I just need to slap on some lip gloss, then I'll head over to one of those agencies."

Another lie. Hayato was going to hit the manga café and drown his panic in stories about pirates and gay sex.

6

M asuo arrived at his parlor an hour before it opened. Deep down he'd hoped a few people would be standing outside, but the only thing waiting for Masuo was the cold.

Unlocking the parlor didn't give him the same warmth it had the day before, even with Daichi's charm attached to the chain. Stepping inside no longer filled him with hope. Instead, reality hit him harder than a winter's storm. He pulled out his list of morning activities and scratched off opening the door. The smaller the task, the easier to complete, and he needed an early win.

An unsettling musk lingered in the air. Masuo narrowed his eyes and squatted next to the biggest of the mysterious stains on the carpet. He pressed his nose against the matted fibers and sniffed. A pungent rusted-iron odor flooded his nose.

Blood.

He fell back on his ass and got his first real look at the yellow patches on the ceiling. He stood and followed the lines of patches down the wall where they'd been painted an off shade of green in a vain attempt to match the lime-colored walls. He rubbed his palm over one of the patches, and the plaster broke away until the outline of a round hole remained.

Bullet holes.

He gulped and backed into one of the pachinko machines. All summer the Kyoto yakuza had fought against a Korean mafia faction called the Double Moon. Masuo had been considered too new a recruit to join the battles and too senior to directly deal with any cleanup. If the previous manager had been gunned down in the parlor, Masuo would honor him by bringing it back to its full glory.

First on his list was replacing the carpet. Hopefully, the day after New Year's was popular enough for pachinko players for him to actually earn the money to replace the carpet. Maybe he could try steam cleaning the stain first.

Masuo spent the rest of the hour picking up some air freshener at the corner store and spraying it all over the parlor until it smelled like spring at a neglected bathhouse. He turned on all the machines, popped in some earplugs to block the noise, and opened the doors to the world.

Morning turned to afternoon, and then an older gentleman entered. His lips were stained from his lunch, and he held a cigarette between his fingers. He exchanged some money for balls and sank into a taped seat in front of a machine.

Finally hearing the metal balls bounce around made Masuo's chest swell. For the first time, it felt real. He was a yakuza and finally fit someplace in the family. Masuo tried not to appear too eager, walking by only once before going to stand behind the prize display case.

"Hey, kid." The man whistled.

Masuo had turned twenty in November. He wasn't a kid anymore. Still, he marched over. "Yes, sir?"

"What happened to Mr. Suzuki? Is he in the back?"

Masuo couldn't say the dark stain on the floor was what was left of Mr. Suzuki.

"He retired," Masuo said.

The man said nothing more, and Masuo awkwardly returned to the prize case.

The man stayed for about an hour before losing all his balls and leaving. It meant some profit for the parlor but not enough to pay the electric bill.

The remaining late-afternoon hours faded to early evening, and at six, Hayato strolled inside. His hair wasn't as styled as yesterday, but something made his eyes glow like shards of amber. Maybe he'd put on eyeliner, or maybe the lights of the machines made them pop, but whatever it was pierced Masuo's heart and brought him back to the soft glow of Hayato's skin underneath the pink lights of the love hotel. The lascivious way he'd parted his legs while Masuo nipped at his inner thigh.

Hayato clanked a metal briefcase onto the display case. A handcuff dangled from the briefcase's handle and connected via a short chain to a cuff around Hayato's wrist.

"So you are into the kinky stuff," Masuo blurted out.

"You don't know the half of it."

Masuo bit his tongue before he could say anything else, but it didn't stop more memories from surfacing.

Hayato's sweet moans, his skin burning beneath Masuo's hands. Even if Hayato was a jerk, Masuo couldn't help but be attracted to him.

Hayato gestured to the empty parlor. "Is there even any money in your safe?"

"It's the first day."

"Exactly. The grand opening. Did you even put an ad in the newspaper?"

"Like that would even work."

"If you do it right, it does. Take notes on the people who come in and aim for the papers and magazines for that demographic. Start a social media account. Find a cute mascot for the parlor and take daily photos of it in different locations. Or are you worried about breaking something else?"

Masuo crossed his arms. He didn't have to respond to the cheap jab.

Hayato tapped his fingers on the counter. "Did you set up the phone?"

"Of course I did."

Hayato stepped behind the counter and opened the office door like he owned the place. He picked up the corded phone on the desk and dialed a number. Masuo leaned against the doorframe, his heart speeding up. Hayato couldn't be calling Endo to announce the lack of profits, could he? It was the first day. What did they expect? An overflowing safe with enough cash to make up for all the days the parlor had been closed?

Hayato twisted his finger around the cord while the phone rang. A small crease crossed his brow.

"Hello?" the voice on the other end of the line came through loud enough for Masuo to hear.

"Oh, so when it's a number you don't recognize, you finally pick up." Hayato's caustic tone piqued Masuo's attention. "Don't you fucking dare hang up on me, Jiro, or I swear I'll walk over to the tiny office you have at Sunrise Electrics and make sure everyone there knows your dick has been all over this yakuza ass. Then you can kiss your promotion into upper middle management goodbye. Do I have your attention now?"

Masuo turned away so he could pretend he wasn't listening.

"I want my stuff back," Hayato said. "Put it in a box outside the apartment and tell me when to get it."

"Don't come anywhere near the apartment, or I'll call the police!" Jiro screamed.

Hayato's ex sounded like a jerk. No wonder they had been together. Jerks attracted jerks. Whatever. Not Masuo's problem.

"Can I at least have the picture back?" Hayato's voice had lowered in desperation. "Hello, Jiro? Are you there? Jiro!"

Masuo shook his head. Why did he feel bad for Hayato? The man had called him an idiot. The picture was probably a nude. It was Hayato's own damn fault for sending them to someone untrustworthy.

Hayato slammed the phone back into the cradle and groaned.

Masuo grinned. "So you got back with your boyfriend?"

"I dumped his ass." Pain laced Hayato's words.

He was shit at hiding his emotions. It was almost sad.

An uncomfortable lump formed in Masuo's throat.

No. He refused to feel bad for Hayato. He was a jerk. Still, even jerks could be defenseless.

"Wanna go for a drink or something?" Masuo asked.

Hayato pointed to the briefcase. "Unlike yours, the other parlors actually make money."

"I mean after you're done."

Hayato rolled his eyes. "I have enough going on right now, and I don't want to listen to your lame pickup lines so you can relive some New Year's fantasy."

"It's not like that."

"Uh-huh." Hayato glanced down.

Masuo knew he wasn't hard, but he checked anyway. Hayato laughed. Bastard.

Masuo crossed his arms. "Aren't you a yakuza? Shouldn't it be easy for you to get your stuff back?"

"Aren't you a yakuza? Shouldn't it be easy for you to get people to gamble?"

Masuo's mouth opened, but no words came out. His face grew hot, and he wished he could've been anywhere but there with Hayato staring at him in disgust.

"That's what I thought." Hayato grabbed his briefcase. "Do better tomorrow."

Hayato walked out, and Masuo didn't mean to stare at Hayato's ass, but he did. Masuo pressed his fist against his palm.

Everything about Hayato pissed Masuo off. Especially how when they were together, Masuo immediately thought of their New Year's evening in each other's arms Whatever had happened between the party that night and Hayato crawling on the floor to look for his underwear the next morning was better left forgotten.

Still, Hayato thought Masuo was an idiot, and he

needed to prove himself. He was a good yakuza and deserved the same level of respect as all the other parlor managers. He knew just how to earn it.

Masuo pulled out his phone and called Arashi.

"You free tonight?" Masuo asked.

"You wanna get drinks?"

"Maybe after, but first I need your help playing dress-up."

7

M asuo and Arashi stood outside Hayato's sleek tower of an apartment building. It couldn't have been more than a few years old and probably charged rent to match its height. No one needed a doorman at midnight, but there one stood in the freezing cold. Poor guy.

"This is going to be fun," Arashi said.

Masuo swept back his hair and returned the police cap to his head. "Glad you think so. It wouldn't be half as fun alone."

The police uniforms had been easy to get. No one would question the wrong shade of blue or look long enough to discover the badges were cheap plastic. Acting the part mattered most, and Masuo knew how to pretend.

They strolled through the door and into the swanky lobby. The floors shined so much, and he could see Arashi grinning like he owned the place.

"Damn." He whistled. "When do we get paid enough to afford a place like this?"

Masuo shook his head. "What apartment is it?"

"One, one, two."

"First floor. That makes it easy."

Arashi had gotten Hayato's address from an "in case of emergency" checklist. Masuo hadn't gotten one, or maybe it was somewhere in the desk drawers he hadn't had the heart to clean out.

They strolled past the hallway of elevators and into a corridor, but instead of leading to apartment twelve, it led to offices.

Arashi shrugged. "Must be floor eleven, apartment two, then."

Masuo blinked. Eleven? What kind of madman made an apartment building with eleven floors? Didn't the Kyoto ordinance limit obscenely tall buildings?

Arashi pushed the elevator button. Masuo rubbed his hands against his slacks and cleared his throat. He could do it. Eleven wasn't too bad.

The doors opened. Arashi stepped inside the elevator car, but Masuo's feet remained stuck to the floor.

"Come on," Arashi said. "It's just an elevator. This one's even bigger than most."

It was still the middle of the night. What would happen if they got stuck? Who would come for them? The power could go off, and they could fall all eleven floors to their death. New constructions always cut corners. They'd probably left out all the safety devices to come in under budget.

Arashi sighed. "You've got to get over this sometime."

The doors closed, and Masuo could think straight again. The stairs stood beside the elevators. He had no other option.

Masuo's short breaths echoed through the concrete coffin that was the stairway. He clutched onto the cold metal railing and took his first step. The stairs might've been better than an elevator, but it didn't mean they were easy.

He had to do it. He had to prove himself to Hayato, and the fastest way to do that was to do something he couldn't.

Masuo could imagine the look on Hayato's face already. His plump glossed lips opened wide in shock. His gaze would soften, and he'd look at Masuo with the same awe he had when Masuo had made him come for the third time. Masuo swallowed and took the first flight of stairs with his eyes closed, his heart bouncing in his chest like a pachinko jackpot.

By the eleventh floor, Masuo's breaths were short and shallow. He stood outside the stairwell door and took a few deep breaths so he wouldn't look like a weakling in front of Arashi.

Masuo opened the door, and Arashi was waiting for him.

"You need a second?" Arashi asked.

Masuo flexed his arms. "Eleven floors were nothing. You ready for this?"

"I've been practicing my bad cop persona."

"What happens if I want to play bad cop?"

Arashi shrugged. "Then there're two bad cops. The ex sounds like he deserves it."

"Sounds like a plan." Masuo knocked on the door. "Police."

No answer.

"Police, open up." Masuo deepened his voice, making it low and threatening.

A lock turned, and the man Masuo assumed was Jiro opened the door. His short hair stuck up in serious bed head. His striped button-up pajamas were comically conservative. How had such an obvious corporate slug ended up with Hayato?

Masuo flashed his badge. "We're with the organized crime unit."

Jiro's face turned red, and he cleared his throat. "I don't know how much help I'd be, officer. I'm a simple salaryman."

Arashi pushed open the door and made his way inside. "I think you have information we need or else we wouldn't be here."

Masuo followed and pulled out a small notepad from his pocket. He turned to a random page, pretending to read. "It says here you are in contact with one Hayato Kobayashi."

"Maybe as a passing acquaintance, but the name isn't familiar."

"Then why are his possessions here?" Arashi pointed to a random fuzzy purple cushion. It was the brightest thing in the minimalist room.

"I-I..." Jiro's eyes went as large as five-hundred-yen coins. "I was so scared. I couldn't even bring myself to touch his things. Once I learned he was yakuza, I completely disconnected from him."

Masuo rolled his eyes. "He has a dragon tattoo on his back. How could you think he wasn't a yakuza?"

"I thought it was a twin thing. His brother is a bouncer or something and has the same one."

"And the huge scar on his stomach?"

"He told me he had his appendix removed." There was panic in Jiro's voice. "I was away on a work trip when it happened. I didn't know. I swear."

Masuo laughed. "The law makes it very clear. Citizens are not to have relationships with yakuza. You work at Sunrise Electrics, right? I'm sure they wouldn't like to know one of their workers keeps yakuza among his friends."

Arashi nodded along. "The company has some government deals they are looking to bid on. It wouldn't look good if your relationship with a yakuza was brought up."

"Please don't tell the company heads! I kicked Hayato out. Changed the locks and everything! He's not in my life anymore."

Masuo clicked his tongue and glanced around the room. "Keeping so much of his stuff doesn't look like you're trying to dissociate. We'll be happy to dispose of Hayato's items, for a fee, of course."

Jiro's hand shook as he grabbed his wallet from the coffee table. Arashi glared at him, looking as intimidating as someone with a pop idol's face could. Still, Jiro's Adam's apple bobbed as he gulped and handed his thick wallet to Masuo.

Jackpot.

Masuo pocketed the large stack of cash and dropped the wallet on the ground. The wad of bills meant he could get the parlor carpet replaced.

He whistled to Arashi. "Let's go. Clear it out."

"Thank you, officers!"

Jiro fell to his knees and pointed to a paperweight on

the table. It was shaped like a popsicle made from brains. It was kind of cute in a creepy way.

"That horrible thing is his," Jiro said.

"Suitcase?" Arashi grunted.

"I've got a few in here."

Masuo grabbed the brain freeze pop figure and followed Jiro to the bedroom. He pulled two suitcases from underneath the bed: one was bright pink with neon-green flowers, and the other was black. Clearly the vibrant one was Hayato's. Masuo unzipped it and put the paperweight inside.

"Everything in this closet is his too," Jiro said.

Arashi grabbed an armful of clothes and put them in the case. Masuo took a step to help, but then a picture frame caught his attention. Masuo plucked the polished silver frame off the nightstand.

A woman stood underneath a blooming cherry tree with twin boys holding each of her hands. Their features matched, so the woman had to be the boys' mother. They looked about six, and the little uniforms and backpacks probably meant it was their first day of school. One of them had to be Hayato, but the boys looked identical down to their bowl cuts.

Hayato didn't seem sentimental enough to keep an old family photo next to his bed.

Masuo's eyes narrowed. What kind of an ass was Jiro for not returning Hayato's family photo?

Masuo pulled Arashi aside and whispered, "Jiro's an ass. Fill the second suitcase with crap that's going to inconvenience him as much as the bastard inconvenienced Hayato."

Arashi chuckled and took the second suitcase into the

other room. Jiro didn't even notice, instead he fidgeted, neatly folding Hayato's clothes. Surprisingly, they were not as colorful as Masuo had imagined. Hayato must've kept it to his underwear.

Masuo shook his head. "You seriously had no idea?"

"I swear. He never talked about his work, but he'd always ask about mine."

Or Jiro was too full of himself to even bother asking Hayato.

"How long were you two living together?" Masuo asked.

"About two years," Jiro said.

"Any of the furniture his?"

"I lived here before, and he moved in."

Masuo raised a brow. "When did he move in?"

"About a month after we met."

Hayato moved in with a scared little wimp after a month but had had the best sex in years with Masuo and wouldn't give him his number?

"I didn't know he was a yakuza." Jiro returned to pleading. "Hayato has more lip gloss than I have ties. How could I have known?"

Masuo's skin burned. What had Hayato seen in someone like Jiro? Some boring salaryman who was too scared to realize he was being conned.

Hayato had held Masuo's hand all fucking night. Through every twist, every turn, Hayato clutched on like they were eternal lovers. When Masuo had woken with their fingers laced together, he'd never felt so needed, so desperately connected to someone in his life. But now it felt like a plague instead of a blessing.

"What else is his?" Masuo asked between clenched teeth.

The makeup.

The contacts.

The perfume.

Hayato had better be fucking grateful for each thing Masuo lovingly packed.

Arashi whistled from the living room, stuffed black suitcase in hand.

"If we have any trouble, you'll hear back from us." Masuo's voice was flat and stern.

Arashi gave a final grunt.

They headed out, Arashi taking the suitcases into the elevator and Masuo taking the stairs.

Hayato followed the apartment manager into the staged bedroom. The closet would hold all his clothes, even the ones still hanging in Jiro's closet.

Hayato hated to admit it, but Masuo had a point. Hayato was a yakuza. He should've been able to grab Jiro by the collar and force him to open the door. Instead, Hayato had avoided the uncomfortable conversation and had gone shopping, thinking it would all blow over in a few days. Too bad he couldn't avoid moving into a new place.

"What floor is the available unit on?" Hayato asked.

"The seventh."

The model was on the fifth floor, and the street traffic hummed at the same frequency as the refrigerator. Not good. His old place on the eleventh floor had contained no reminders of the existence of humanity below, and it had also come with a boyfriend to prevent loneliness from sinking into Hayato's marrow.

"It'll be available this Friday?" Hayato asked.

"That won't be any trouble at all."

"Awesome."

Nothing could be further from awesome. The obligation to allow his brother to start a life detached from him weighed down Hayato like concrete shoes. If responsibility were an ocean, Hayato would've drowned long ago.

"I'll be in the office if you need anything. I know most people like to take some time to look around without feeling rushed."

The manager left, and Hayato plopped down on the sofa decorated with enough pillows that he risked accidental smothering. The apartment hit everything on his wish list. The perfect distance from the parlors, his brother, and his favorite bar. It was newly built and Western-style. Nothing he could say no to.

He might as well get it over with and sign a lease agreement. He stood, his joints snapping.

Then the silence closed in.

He was alone.

The ceiling fan resembled the one from his childhood home. White. In the center of the living room. Each time he opened the door, the fan would be the first thing he'd see. Exactly like his childhood home. Exactly like that day when he was ten. But Subaru wouldn't be there yelling at him not to look.

Hayato staggered back, but the tide of his thoughts had already tossed him out into the violent sea. Being alone was dangerous. People did stupid things when they were alone. No one would be there to stop him.

The doorknob stabbed him in the back. Hayato's fingers shook as he groped for the handle. His throat closed, the breath growing stale in his mouth. He ran, but it didn't stop the memories from chasing after him.

He escaped the building, but his thrashing heart didn't slow until he became part of the crowd. Shoulder to shoulder with others, the memory of the worst day of his life faded like a ship sinking to the bottom of the sea. His heart slowed to a steady rhythm.

Hayato encouraged himself with each step. He was surrounded by others. People would stop him if he tried to do something stupid. He wasn't alone, and everything was perfect.

He followed the stream of people to the train station. His favorite twenty-four-hour manga café stood among the storefronts. Rows and rows of manga lined the front entry. Everything from *One Piece* to the latest volume of Hayato's favorite gay series, *My Master's Wish*. He grabbed enough volumes to keep his mind afloat until work rescued him. A few hours with the books and the short partition wall that separated him from his neighbor but still allowed him to see someone was there would dispel the last of Hayato's loneliness.

THE HANDCUFF CHAIN clanked against Hayato's metal briefcase. No matter how many layers he wore, the cuff always sent a cold shock up his arm like he'd been stabbed with an icicle. At least it wasn't raining yet.

Masuo's parlor had a few more people in it than it had had the day before. Still not enough to make it worth Hayato's time. At some point, he needed to show Masuo the ropes, but with everything going on, Masuo sat low on his priority list.

Oh well. Masuo was fun to tease if nothing else. Though today the pinstriped vest he wore hugged his body in all the right places. The sharp lines of his crisp white collar emphasized his neck and sharp jaw. In a few years, the last of Masuo's boyish features would turn into the fully chiseled face of a man. He wouldn't be able to walk down the street without turning heads. A part of Hayato wished he could remember New Year's. It might've been a bright patch in the depressing month.

Hayato set the briefcase on the prize counter and tapped his fingers against the metal.

"You're early," Masuo said.

"I'm full of surprises." Hayato winked. He couldn't help but flirt.

"I'll keep that in mind. I have money for you today."

"Maybe you're not so incompetent after all."

Hayato followed Masuo into the office. On top of the desk were his and Jiro's suitcases. Hayato's jaw dropped. He unzipped his suitcase, exposing his neatly folded clothes.

"How did you get all my stuff back?" Hayato dug around in the suitcase even though the briefcase chained to his wrist made the process cumbersome. "Everything's here. Everything! From the brain freeze statue down to my favorite lip gloss."

Masuo leaned against the doorframe, a well-deserved smug smile across his face. He wouldn't be so bad if he could rein in his pride, but Masuo grinned like every cheeky early twentysomething who'd somehow managed to do the right thing.

Hayato had never been that bad, had he? No. Subaru would never have allowed him to be so cocky.

"So you know how to fetch, but you're still not good at getting people to hand you money." Hayato uncapped a pale-rose gloss and dabbed it across his lips. "Maybe you should try stripping."

Masuo shook his head. He was so easy to tease, and he looked too damn cute when he pretended he could take it.

"Keep looking," Masuo said. "If you're still missing something, I can go back and get it for you. I know you had a hard time getting your stuff back."

Oh, so he did have a little fight in him. Like one of those fuzzy little dogs that barked a whole bunch but were smaller than pigeons and not nearly as brave as they seemed.

Hayato fanned through his suit jackets and his sweaters, but one was thick and unmoving with something tucked inside. He reached inand pulled out the framed photograph of his mom. A brightness coiled around him, banishing the swirl of heaviness January brought. It might've been small, just a photograph, but it stood like a lighthouse in the raging storm inside Hayato. He pressed his lips together and hugged the frame.

"I..." Hayato's words faded like a memory better left forgotten. "Thank you.

Masuo shrugged. "It was only right for you to have your stuff back. I'm glad I could help."

He could've easily teased back, demanding Hayato speak louder and repeat his thank-you, but Masuo didn't. The curved lines of his smirk softened like he'd felt Hayato's painful plea to keep back the loneliness.

Hayato shook his head. No. He didn't need another man to scoop him out of his solitude. It was time he learned to make it on his own.

"What's in the other suitcase?" Hayato asked. "I like shopping, but I don't have that many clothes."

Masuo laughed even though Hayato knew his joke wasn't that funny, but it lightened the mood. "I figured Jiro made life super inconvenient for you, so I nabbed some stuff that would make life super inconvenient for him."

Hayato unzipped the other suitcase. It held a sundries store worth of items. Jiro's toothbrush, a handful of his dull-ass ties, all his left shoes. Jiro was going to be so pissed, and Hayato loved it!

He moved the collection of spoons aside and found a tall black box.

"You snagged Jiro's bottle of Dom Pérignon! His boss gave him that when he saved the company a ton by firing a whole team and replacing them with contractors. He kept saying how he'd open it on a special occasion. Our first anniversary? Not enough. Me getting a promotion? Not enough. Ugh, he was such a loser." Hayato pulled the bottle out of its box. "You got any glasses?"

"Coffee mugs count?"

"Perfect." Hayato grinned. "Jiro would be even more pissed if he knew we were drinking his prized champagne from coffee cups."

Masuo grabbed some mugs with the parlor's logo on them.

Hayato ripped the foil from the bottle. "Get behind me so it doesn't hit you in the eye."

He twisted off the wire cage and popped the cork. Champagne gushed out.

"Hurry, get the glasses!" Hayato said.

It was too late. Half the champagne had spilled all over them, but Hayato couldn't remember the last time he'd laughed so hard. The sweet tang of flowers and berries lingered in the air. His fingers sticky, dirty, and ready for more.

Hayato licked the champagne off his fingers and grabbed a mug out of Masuo's hand. Their gazes met, and Hayato's heart beckoned the other man closer.

Masuo's sandy-brown eyes closed, and he leaned in, ready to share a kiss. Hayato's heart screamed at him to do it. His fingers ached for another's touch. His lips already buzzed with the excitement.

The kiss would swallow him whole, and he could fall into the trance of beauty and sex. A whole month in a surreal fantasy of endorphins. The longing clung to Hayato like his favorite pair of pants, but he swallowed and pulled himself out of his desire.

Hayato put his finger up to Masuo's ready lips.

"Hey now, don't ruin my lip gloss," Hayato warned.

"Sorry, I didn't..." Masuo pulled back and looked at the floor.

Masuo was cute and sexy, and maybe there was more behind his cocky grin. Hayato could easily see them together, but at the same time, Hayato could just as easily see himself with one of the parlor customers out front. January jumbled all his thoughts, and his heart cried out for mercy from his solitude more than any other time of the year. If he wasn't careful, he'd end up in another mismatched relationship that would end in disaster.

But that didn't mean he couldn't have fun. He owed Masuo a thank-you and maybe an apology for being an ass the past few days.

"I'll be back when you close tonight," Hayato said. "Then we can celebrate getting my wardrobe back in style. That work for you?"

"I'll be waiting."

9

———————

Masuo pulled his piercing back through his lip and tugged off his tie. Then he unbuttoned the top three buttons of his shirt, exposing a nice amount of chest.

"Maybe too much," Masuo mumbled to himself, deciding two would be fine and three made him look desperate.

He wanted to be perfect for his date with Hayato.

Was it a date? It felt like a date. It was probably better Masuo didn't think it was a date, especially since Hayato had rejected the perfect kissable moment. He shouldn't have even tried, but everything had felt so right. A kiss would've made it all the sweeter.

Masuo shook the champagne-filled fantasy out of his head and slid on his jacket. He waited for Hayato outside the parlor. Hopefully he hadn't been joking about going for a drink, intending to leave Masuo waiting out in the cold.

It didn't take long for Hayato to stroll up. Masuo's

mouth dropped open. Hayato had ditched the typical yakuza suit and tie and wore a black coat with fuzzy trim. It draped across him like a short dress. A light layer of makeup emphasized his lush pink lips, and glittery purple eyeshadow made his amber eyes pop.

"Your eyes are so big," Masuo blurted out. He needed to learn to control his mouth around Hayato.

"Don't be too impressed. They're contacts." Hayato laughed. "Thanks again for rescuing my favorite honey-colored lens collection. They were limited edition, and I've been feeling naked without them."

Masuo had no idea what Hayato was talking about, but he could've said anything, and it would've been fine. He was there, and that was all that mattered.

"I know a place. Wanna go there?" Hayato asked.

"Whatever you want."

Hayato winked. "That's what I like to hear."

Masuo followed Hayato down the street. An electronic buzz sparked like a string of firecrackers through Masuo's body. Damn the way Hayato's jacket framed his ass in his tight pants. Was he wearing underwear?

Hayato stopped and looked over his shoulder. "Why don't you walk beside me. That way you'll stop checking out my ass and start a conversation."

"I wasn't—"

"You think I can't tell?"

Masuo laughed and stepped to Hayato's side.

"Well, you do have a nice ass," Masuo said.

"That's the kind of conversation I like. Keep talking."

"And a nice smile."

"Go on."

"And you can be kind of a jerk."

Hayato opened his mouth, then his lips curled into a smile. "I promise I'm not a jerk."

"So you say."

"I'm your boss."

"So that means it's okay you're a jerk?"

"Okay, maybe I've been more of a hard-ass with you than with others. I'm sorry about that." Hayato sighed. "January is a hard month."

All the parlors must have lower profits in January. Knowing Endo, she probably blamed it on Hayato, who had to push all the managers.

"You can go back to complimenting me if you want," Hayato offered.

Masuo laughed. "Three things seems enough."

"I only count two unless you're trying to tell me calling me a jerk was a compliment."

"Well, I didn't call you an asshole." Masuo grinned. "Still, I'm excited to see how you make it up to me. I did rescue your circle lenses collection."

"I'll buy the drinks today, then we're even."

"Deal."

Hayato took them to a gay bar so tiny Masuo could stretch out his arms and touch both sides. Eight people and the place looked packed.

Everyone greeted Hayato, exchanging air kisses and inside jokes. He returned each greeting with the same warmth given. There was the Hayato Masuo had met at New Year's. Open and eager to make sure everyone had a good time. Masuo scurried to the empty stool beside Hayato before someone else could take it.

Masuo strummed his fingers against the electric-blue Lucite bar. "You come here often, I take it?"

"Hayato visits every week," the bartender answered, turning to Hayato. "You want your usual?"

"Yeah, and keep them coming. Get one for my friend too." Hayato turned to Masuo. "Jiro would always stay late at work on Wednesdays to prepare for his Thursday meeting. I'd get bored and would come here until he came home."

Masuo nodded, still on the high of Hayato introducing him as a friend. It had to mean something. He wasn't an incompetent underling but a friend.

The bartender brought over two bright-blue drinks. "You usually never come on Saturdays. Is Jiro on a business trip?"

"I dumped his boring ass." There was pain in Hayato's voice. He held up his glass and turned to Masuo. "Here. Let's toast to finally getting my stuff back and to your parlor. Hopefully it'll have better profits tomorrow."

They clinked their glasses together, and Masuo drank the sweet-and-salty drink.

"Do you like your drink?" Hayato asked.

"It's delicious."

"I know. I could drink a dozen of them without realizing. So, are you gay, bi, pan..."

"Bi," Masuo gave a half smile. "Hopefully you're not one of those guys who thinks it's disgusting that I've been with a woman."

"Nah. I've slept with plenty of drag queens."

"That's not exactly—"

Hayato waved his hand and took another gulp of his drink. "You know what I mean."

Masuo didn't.

Hayato was already halfway done with his drink, while Masuo was on his second sip.

"Do you prefer men or women more?" Hayato asked.

Masuo rubbed his thumb against the side of his glass. He'd never gone into details with anyone before, but Hayato made his sexuality abundantly clear, and something about that relaxed Masuo and made him feel like he could finally be himself.

"I've always preferred men," Masuo said. "Growing up, I never thought it could happen, so I always hid that part of myself and went out with girls. Even when a boy confessed he liked me, I completely rejected him. But then I heard Father Murata was gay. He's such a badass and doesn't care if anyone knows he sleeps with men. If he could do it, then so could I. Nothing will stop me from getting married and having kids with someone I love. Woman or man."

Hayato burst out laughing. "Except the LDP running things. Gay marriage will never be legal, and you do know two men can't have kids, right?"

"There's all that talk in Shibuya about allowing gay marriage."

"Not having kids is the best part about being with a man. Are you even out to your parents?"

"Not yet."

"Well, Mr. I Like to Write Lists, coming out to your parents should be your number one. After that disaster, you'll see how you can't simply scratch off wife and put husband on your idea of domestic bliss. Is that what made you join the yakuza in the first place? Thinking you could help change things?"

Masuo shook his head. "Is that your favorite pickup line?"

"I don't have to use a pickup line on you. You already want me."

Masuo pressed his lips together. It was true. Still, they'd already had the "why did you join the yakuza" conversation at the New Year's party. Maybe Hayato had been so drunk then he couldn't remember it.

"I was in a bad earthquake as a kid," Masuo said. "Part of the building slipped off its foundation. I was trapped in an elevator. A yakuza saved me before anyone in the government had even shown up. Since then, I always wanted to be a yakuza and help the defenseless like they helped me."

"Really?" Hayato laughed and downed the rest of his drink. "You take all that white-knight shit seriously?"

Masuo's eyes narrowed. "I'm living proof it's true."

"Fine, fine."

"What made you want to join?"

"I didn't tell you before?"

"No, you said how it must've been lonely trapped in there, then asked my favorite sex position."

"I'm versatile." Hayato winked.

Masuo bit his tongue, trying not to get frustrated. "Why did you join the yakuza?"

"The money's good."

"That's it? Money?"

Hayato stared at Masuo as if daring him to ask for the truth, but Masuo kept his gaze, wanting to see beneath the makeup and contacts. Hayato broke first, grabbing his new drink and taking a gulp. When he pulled down the glass, his eyes glowed as if daring Masuo to listen.

"My mom left us when I was ten." Hayato's ring tapped against his empty glass. "It hit Dad pretty hard, but he got remarried when my brother and I were fifteen. We only met her a few months before the wedding, but it was clear she didn't want to suddenly have to deal with two teenage boys. Subaru suggested that Dad let us rent an apartment so he and his wife could start their life together.

"It worked well for a few years, then we got a notice the rent was late. Turned out Dad had had a baby and couldn't afford our rent anymore. Of course, he forgot to tell us." Hayato rolled his eyes. "Subaru's older, by three minutes, and decided it was his job to work while I finished school. He even made me take the college entrance exams and everything."

Hayato's words sat in Masuo's stomach like a lead weight. First Hayato's mom had abandoned him, then his dad. Masuo might've been trapped in an elevator, but outside, his mother called out to him. Even when he joined the yakuza, both his parents still wanted to see him. He had to call every few weeks or his mom worried.

"But that explains why Subaru joined, not you," Masuo said.

"Could you imagine my gay ass on a construction site?" Hayato laughed and finished off his drink. "Being a yakuza was a lot easier. Maybe not during the war, but that's behind us now. And the only other job where I could be this gay is as a go-go dancer. A guy calls me a fag here, then I beat the shit out of him. Now with Father Murata as godfather, no one would dare act homophobic."

The hours passed, but Masuo couldn't tell until he

yawned and looked at the clock. Hayato opened up more as the drinks flowed. Even the silent pauses in their conversations were comfortable, like the deep connection of a relationship decades old.

"Last drink," Masuo said after his third. He'd lost count how many Hayato had finished. "I have to wake up early to open tomorrow."

"Okay, okay." Hayato held up his drink. "To all the fun things I get to do now that I am single!"

They tapped their glasses together.

"Like what?" Masuo asked.

"Really good phone sex. No videos or pictures. That's cheating. It needs to be where you make up what you're wearing and all that stuff. Jiro wouldn't even send me a photo of him shirtless when he'd go on business trips."

"I always wanted to go into one of those super expensive apartment showings pretending I was going to buy it."

Hayato laughed. "That is the dullest fantasy I've ever heard. Come on, Masuo, live a little. What have you secretly always wanted?"

"You want something sexy?"

"The sexier, the better. I want to know all your fantasies."

"Let's make a list."

Masuo took out a little notebook and on a blank page, wrote his house tour at the top of one side, then Hayato's phone sex beside it.

"Matching piercings," Masuo said, then wrote it underneath the house tour.

"What?" Hayato shook his head. "That's not sexy. That's painful."

"It can be very erotic, especially if it's in a more sensitive location."

Hayato clicked his tongue, clearly not impressed. "Next, I want to be jacked off on a busy train."

"Very risqué."

"Now you have to give a sexy one." Hayato playfully poked Masuo. "It's not fair that I keep giving you good ones, and you give ones I'd never want to do."

"Getting breakfast in bed—"

"That's not sexy."

"Naked," Masuo finished.

"Okay, not bad, but you've slept with women and need to step up your definition of kinky with me. We'll work on that."

Hayato leaned over, his head on Masuo's shoulder. His heart bounced around his chest like the balls flying around a pachinko machine. The light buzz of alcohol almost made Hayato glow, and the soft flush on his face reminded Masuo they were both very drunk again. Last time they'd both been drunk like this, it had led to the best sex of his life.

"You know what I've wanted for years now?" Hayato said.

"What?"

Hayato cupped his hand around Masuo's ear and whispered, "I've always wanted to be arrested and have to *convince* the cop to let me go with my mouth."

An almost undetectable gasp left Masuo, but the grin on Hayato's face meant he'd heard. He turned in his seat, his legs spreading Masuo's.

"Are you going to write that down?" Hayato asked as if it was a come-on.

Masuo swallowed and wrote.

Hayato stared down at Masuo's lap before slowly lifting his gaze. "You want to get out of here? Maybe check out another hotel?"

Masuo refrained from saying yes. He'd finally started to get to know Hayato without flashing back to their New Year's sex adventure. Another few rounds of sex wouldn't help Masuo learn anything about Hayato outside the bedroom.

"I gotta open tomorrow." Masuo hoped he wouldn't regret his decision in the morning. "Some of us don't have the pleasure of starting work after dinner."

"You have to get some scars before you earn the privilege."

"But can I at least have your number now?" Masuo could kick himself for sounding so insecure.

Hayato held up a finger. "Only call if you're ready for phone sex."

"As ready as I'll ever be."

"Good enough."

Hayato wrote his number on the top of the list. Masuo pocketed it and smiled. It was a real date. His first real date with a man, and Masuo couldn't have asked for anyone sexier.

"Walk you back to the station?" Masuo offered.

"Only if I get to stare at your ass this time."

Hayato groped for his ringing phone. Stupid noise. Had he set his alarm? He could barely remember most of last night, let alone if he'd been sober enough to set an alarm when he'd got home. Fucking hangover. Why did January suck so much?

"Who is it?" Subaru mumbled.

Somehow Hayato managed to find his phone behind the photo of their mom. He answered, not even checking the caller ID.

"Hello?" Hayato kept his voice low.

"I'm calling to take care of your morning load."

"What?"

"Your morning load." Masuo's voice finally clicked in Hayato's head.

It was *not* okay to call someone before noon. If Masuo thought Hayato had been a jerk before—

Masuo continued. "I'm sure you only need to look down to know what I'm talking about."

Who did Masuo think he was, giving Hayato orders? He pulled back the phone, ready to hang up, but then he spotted the tent in his briefs.

"My morning load," Hayato repeated.

"Hangover slowed your thinking?" Masuo's cheeky grin could be heard in his voice.

"Shut up."

Hayato left the bed and locked himself in the bathroom. It was on the other side of the apartment, so Subaru probably wouldn't hear, but Hayato turned on the faucet just in case.

"What are you wearing?" Masuo's voice was low and husky, tickling Hayato's ear.

He licked his lips. He hadn't had a phone-sex session in ages. Though pink briefs with rainbow trim didn't make for the most sensual role-play.

"You called right in the middle of me getting dressed," Hayato said.

Masuo laughed. "That's such a lie."

"If you don't want to be part of this fantasy, I can hang up and enjoy it on my own."

"Are you a pants-first or shirt-first kind of guy?" Masuo changed his tune fast.

"I got the last button of my shirt done. I was about to pick what pants to wear."

Hayato hummed and sat on the side of the tub. In such a tiny bathroom, if he angled just right, he could catch all of himself in the mirror. He wiggled to get a better view, his briefs riding up. Damn. Subaru might have the bulky muscles, but Hayato had some too. He was a yakuza, after all, and had to keep a workout routine.

He'd wasted his body during his years with Jiro. Hayato's high school sex-ed class had had more variety than Jiro, and that had lasted two days.

Hayato hadn't even really liked him anyway. He was a soggy, limp noodle at the bottom of the bowl, while Masuo already knew exactly what Hayato liked, and they weren't even dating.

"You wearing underwear today or is your cock peeking out from the bottom of your shirt?" Masuo's heavy breath sent Hayato's imagination running.

"I'm working today, so I've got some on," Hayato said.

"Hmm. What kind of fruit is it this time?"

"Not fruit this time, baby." Okay, so not the sexiest, but Hayato was out of practice.

"What is it, then?"

"Eggplant."

A small chuckle came from Masuo, and then Hayato joined. A peaceful sigh left his lips. He hadn't felt so completely himself in ages.

"I got a whole orchard and farm, honey," Hayato added.

"That's ironic, since my boxers have peaches on them."

Their conversation had turned into a morning at the farmer's market.

Hayato rubbed himself through his briefs, keeping the mood. "Have you done this before?"

"Y-yes."

"You're such a bad liar. Let's start over before we swap jam recipes. You still at home or did you get to the parlor?"

"I'm still at home."

"Okay, I'm there too. I pushed you onto the bed. I can see the desire in your eyes. I lean on the bed and put my hand right over your crotch. I can feel you. You already want me." Hayato's hand hovered over his crotch. "Can you feel me?"

"Yeah." Masuo's words were wet and sultry.

"What do you want?"

"I want you to touch me."

"Where?"

"My cock." A sharp gasp came over the line. "Make me hard, Hayato."

Good thing Masuo wasn't shy, even if he was getting ahead of himself playing pretend. Hayato hadn't touched him yet, so there should've been no gasp. A whimpering wine, sure. A *Hayato, you're so big, put it in me,* all the better. But no gasp. Even if Masuo was too eager and had jumped ahead in the fantasy, he provided feedback. The worst phone sex was when the other person was silent as a trip to the library.

"That's what I like to hear." A little moan left the back of Hayato's throat. "I'm unzipping your pants now. I already feel your heat on my hand. I reach inside and pull out your cock. Can you feel me touching you?"

Hayato set his cock free. Imagining his cock was Masuo's admittedly bigger dick, Hayato lavished it with teasingly light touches. Masuo let out a string of breathy moans. Hayato closed his eyes and saw Masuo writhing with pleasure.

"I can feel you touching me," Masuo said. "It feels so good."

Hayato stared at his cock in the mirror and pretended

it was Masuo's. As Masuo's heavy breaths echoed in his ear, a wave of heat flushed through Hayato's body.

"You're leaking at your tip." Hayato's thumb smeared the milky precum leaking out.

Masuo's sweet moans carried off the less desirable feelings wrestling inside Hayato. The pain of January forgotten. The lingering longing for Jiro had been abandoned for Masuo's sheer cries of pleasure and relief.

Hayato lifted himself a little higher, his toes curled, and ready for release.

"Are you close?" Hayato managed to get out.

"Yeah."

"Then tell me when you come. I want to hear it."

Masuo's breathing hitched and got louder and more guttural. Hayato bit his lip, finding the delicate mix of frustration and ecstasy as he got himself so close to the edge of climax he could taste it. He could see Masuo under him, skin glistening underneath a layer of salty sweat. A few stray strands of his black hair sticking to his face. His mouth agape and moans spilling out like precum from his massive cock. The air scented with the musk of pleasure and Masuo's vanilla-and-oak cologne.

"I'm coming," Masuo cried.

Hayato tightened his hand around the base of his stiff length. He squirmed, blocking himself from gaining his own relief. Masuo's hiss of a climax sent a shudder through him.

"You sound so hot," Hayato said.

Masuo's breath slowed, and he gulped down a breath of air. "I'm ready for you to get your eggplant in my peach."

"That's the most unsexy thing anyone has said to me," Hayato said.

"You still hard?"

Masuo had him there.

"I take off your pants and get your peach in the air." Hayato slid off the edge of the tub and dug through the cabinet to find some lube.

Masuo hummed. "And what do you think of my peach?"

"It's begging for me." Damn it. Hayato came up empty. "I'm putting my fingers in your mouth so you can get them nice and wet."

Hayato sucked on two of his fingers, balancing the phone on his shoulder to free up his other hand to continue to stroke himself. Every exploring touch was no different than any other time he'd jacked off, yet images of Masuo, his airy gasps and rippling moans, inundated Hayato and made everything new.

"Hmm." Masuo let out a sloppy sucking sound. "I'm ready for you."

Hayato's fingers popped out of his mouth. "Oh really?"

"Make sure you remember this time."

Hayato pulled down his underwear and angled himself the same way he imagined Masuo, ass in the air, begging to be filled. Hayato was more than happy to please. His finger grazed his entrance.

"Mmm. Stop teasing and hurry up," Masuo said.

"So eager. You're practically swallowing my finger. I have one finger inside. I can feel you trembling with excitement."

Masuo let out a little moan, and Hayato put a finger inside himself, knowing exactly where to angle to hit his spot best. It stung at first, but it was a sweet pain and soon gave rise to pleasure with a few determined thrusts. He dropped the phone to the ground but kept it close so Masuo could hear all Hayato's breaths.

"Give it to me. I can take it," Masuo said. "I already know your body, but I crave you learning all about mine."

"Then let me hear it."

Masuo's aching moan mimicked Hayato's as they played both each other and themselves. The distance between them vanished. They were together. They were one. Their bodies melded. Each gentle touch Hayato lavished on himself, he lavished on Masuo.

"Hmm, you're so tight," Hayato said.

Masuo pleaded for more, harder, faster. Their words strung together. They embraced eternity. Together.

"I'm close. You feel so good." Somehow Hayato's words rang hollow compared to the warmth he felt, the pure surrender.

"Go ahead. Come inside me." Masuo's words rang in Hayato's head like he'd said it himself.

He came, shooting his seed on the floor. His breaths heaved, then slowed as he came down from the high. The blur of their bodies separating. The distance growing. They were apart.

Hayato leaned against the wall and grabbed the phone.

"That was amazing." Hayato's breathing still sounded rough.

"I'm always happy to help."

"Hmm. The white-knight yakuza saving everyone from blue balls."

Masuo laughed. "Maybe just you for that one. I had a nice time last night."

Hayato didn't have the heart to tell him their evening had blurred to black after the third drink. January was such a shit month. Hayato would rather forget it all, even if some good parts happened here and there.

"I'll see you later tonight. Hopefully with some money in your safe," Hayato said.

Masuo gave some lame excuse and said goodbye.

Hayato cleaned up himself and the floor. He shut off the faucet. Hopefully it had masked his moans. He opened the bathroom door and found Subaru awake, sitting up in bed.

"Did the Korean mafia attack again?" Subaru asked.

"Everything's fine." Hayato waved it off. "An apartment manager was calling me back."

"The search is going well, then?"

"Oh yeah. It's wonderful," Hayato lied, even though he knew somehow Subaru could tell. His big-brother powers meant Subaru could read Hayato quicker than a dealer could spot a junkie.

"I know it might be harder for you to find the right place, since it's your first time living alone," Subaru pressed.

Hayato frowned. He only had five days to find a place. It would be hard on anyone.

"I need to get ready to go see another apartment," Hayato said. "Sorry the phone woke you."

"Do you want company?"

Hayato wanted to say yes, but to be perfectly honest,

he wanted to suggest they find a two-bedroom place so all three of them could live together. Yet he couldn't let the foul creature of his selfishness be the barrier to Subaru's happiness. He deserved to move on with his next stage of life. Hayato couldn't keep holding him back.

"Don't worry. I got it," Hayato lied again.

11

M asuo couldn't see himself having another Monday off for the foreseeable future. He needed the mental break after three full days of parlor duties, and he couldn't think of a better way to spend his downtime than helping Kira.

"*Detective Pom Pom!*" Daichi called. "I wanted to watch *Detective Pom Pom.*"

"Okay, *Detective Pom Pom* it is." Masuo clicked over to the daytime children's program.

The theme song for the poodle detective played, and Daichi sang along, mimicking the sound effects. His sister, Sakura, was much more amused by Masuo's cat and brushed the gray tabby's fur.

"Is lunch almost ready?" Masuo called.

"Putting the finishing touches together," Arashi said.

Whenever their days off matched, Arashi would come over and join in the babysitting duties. Though he also had a not-so-secret crush on Kira, and Masuo was sure she was the real reason for the help.

Arashi stepped out of the kitchenette with lunch. The kiddos got octopus-shaped sausages and rabbit-shaped apples, while he and Masuo split the pork cutlet sandwich Arashi had picked up on his way over.

Masuo grabbed his plate. "How much does a new pachinko machine cost?"

"It depends on the machine." Arashi sat beside Masuo on the sofa. "You can usually get some used ones for like two hundred thousand yen."

Masuo jotted down the amount on his notepad. It had been filled with the daily list of parlor duties he'd refer to until it became habit. The back pages were dedicated to figuring out the best way to get the parlor into shape. So far, the ancient machines attracted less people than a pay toilet. He'd stayed up half the night debating whether changing the carpet was more important than updating the machines. Eventually he'd figured if the games were good, no one would notice the bloodstains on the carpet.

"What machines do people like to play most at your parlor?" Masuo asked.

Daichi turned and poked Masuo's shin. "The show's on."

"Sorry," Arashi continued in whispers. "The *Castle Vampire* ones are popular."

"Got it. If I can snag a few used ones on the cheap and then drive some advertising, it could make for a good grand reopening in two weeks."

Arashi took a bite of his sandwich. "Don't you have to close for a grand reopening?"

"Like Endo would ever let me close for two weeks."

"Why don't you ask Hayato?"

Masuo bit his lip. He didn't want to ask for special

treatment, especially since he and Hayato were hitting it off so well. Yesterday, Masuo had been so worried Hayato wouldn't think he was interested anymore because of the love hotel rejection that he'd jumped at the opportunity to call for before-work phone sex. Even if it further complicated their working relationship.

Instead of answering Arashi's question, Masuo avoided it, choosing to become very involved with Detective Pom Pom and the case of the missing sock.

The episode ended, and Masuo cleaned up while Arashi and Daichi played the mysterious case of the missing cat brush over the commercials. Even little Sakura joined in. In the end, the brush had somehow found its way underneath the cat the whole time. Gasp!

Masuo's phone rang.

It was probably Kira needing him to watch the kids for a few more hours. No big deal, especially since it was the last time he could help.

He grabbed his phone, but instead of Kira's name flashing on the screen, it was Hayato's. Hopefully he wasn't expecting another round of phone sex because now was not a good time.

"Hello?" Masuo said.

"Hey, I need you to go somewhere with me," Hayato said.

Masuo wandered into the bedroom. "Where?"

"You'll see."

"So like on a date?"

"More like I need you to help me with something." The tone in Hayato's voice made it sound like a date was the last thing on his mind.

Masuo crossed his arms. Clearly Hayato wasn't ready

for their relationship to become anything more than fun between friends. Masuo had expected their night out would be the spark for a real relationship.

Pain tugged at Masuo's heart. The same pain had echoed in Hayato's voice when he'd talked about Jiro. Two years was a long time. Even if Jiro was a jerk, it would take some time to get used to dating again. Masuo could wait, but he didn't want to be stuck as a fuck buddy. He'd stay with friends until Hayato grew comfortable enough to date him for real. The phone sex had left the ball in Hayato's court.

"Okay," Masuo said. "I can be ready for our not-a-date in about an hour."

"Oh." Hayato sounded shocked Masuo had a life.

"An hour, or I can't do it."

"Fine. An hour, then. I'll text you the address. See you there."

Masuo said his goodbye, and a few moments later an address popped up on his phone.

The next episode of *Detective Pom Pom* played, and Arashi met Masuo in the bedroom. He probably didn't want to get hushed by a child again.

"Who was that?" Arashi asked.

"Hayato."

A dopey smile appeared on Arashi's face. "Still think he's a jerk?"

"He can be a jerk." Masuo nibbled on his lip ring. "But he can be nice when he wants to be."

"Well, he must like you because he never hangs out with the other managers."

Masuo told his heart to stop beating like it was the first time he'd asked a girl on a date in high school.

MASUO SEARCHED the address Hayato had sent him while the train chugged along. A website for some super exclusive-looking apartments popped up. Why would Hayato want to meet him there? Unless they were going to pretend they were looking to live there. Masuo smirked. They might not be on a date, but Hayato was going down Masuo's list. It had to mean there was still hope for a real relationship.

Masuo got off the train and made his way to the luxury tower. It didn't have a doorman, but for some reason, it looked fancier than Jiro's place.

"There you are," Hayato said.

He'd dressed in the typical yakuza suit and tie, but he made the ensemble look so damn hot. His long lashes and rose-glossed lips warmed Masuo on the winter's day.

"Do you think they'll even let me in this place?" Masuo looked down at his black bomber jacket and jeans.

"You'll be fine. Come on."

Hayato's optimism pushed them into the apartment lobby. A huge modern art painting hung behind a sleek glass-topped desk where a lady stood.

"Hey." Hayato took the lead. "I called earlier. I wanted to look at one of your apartments."

"Mr. Kobayashi?" she asked.

"The one and only."

Wasn't Hayato an identical twin?

"Let me call one of our managers, and she'll show you the model. Would you like anything to drink while you wait? We have coffee, wine—"

"Oh, wine, yes. White, red, whatever you've got, I'll take it."

The woman laughed and chatted with Hayato about the wine selection. Masuo's gaze kept bouncing around to the luxury seating and expensive-looking knickknacks left out on side tables. He wasn't from a poor family, but it wasn't like any of the places his parents frequented offered complimentary drinks.

"Would you like anything, sir?"

Masuo's attention snapped back to the woman. "Oh, no. I wouldn't want to trouble you."

Hayato elbowed him. "Come on. Enjoy the full experience."

"I guess a water, then." It sounded the easiest.

"Carbonated? Mineral?"

"Tap is fine."

Hayato didn't hide his amusement with the situation at all. The woman left to get the drinks, and Hayato pulled Masuo to one of the sitting areas. The blue velvet sofa swallowed Masuo when he sat.

"Why do you look like you're about to rob the place?" Hayato playfully whacked Masuo's jiggling leg. "Relax."

"I'm afraid I'm going to break something and spend the next year paying for it."

Hayato laughed. "We're only looking. If you're that worried, cross your arms and pretend nothing impresses you."

"Don't you think the manager would think it's awkward for two guys to look at an apartment together?"

"That's their problem."

"But what if—"

"Being ashamed about your differences makes you

vulnerable. It gives people something they can try to blackmail you with. Show off your difference and use it as a weapon. It'll throw them off and give you the upper hand. People think I'm some limp wrist, but if they mess with me, they'll learn different."

The philosophy must've been how Hayato had survived in the yakuza so long—people underestimated him, and he went above their expectations. Maybe Masuo could use Endo's perception of his incompetence to his advantage.

Masuo nibbled on his lip ring, no longer thinking about taking it out.

The woman came back with Hayato's glass of white wine. She poured a bottle of water into a glass for Masuo and left the half-empty bottle beside it. Even that looked more expensive than his last meal.

Hayato leaned back into the sofa. "This isn't bad at all. What do you think?"

Best to get into character. Masuo crossed his arms. "I don't know. It doesn't even have a doorman like your last place."

"That was especially convenient when I came home with shopping."

They chatted a bit more about silly things.

Hayato finished his glass in time for the manager to greet them.

"I'll be showing you to the model apartment. If you could follow me," she said.

Hayato got up, and Masuo took a few seconds to debate about the water bottle he'd abandoned. It was wasteful to leave it there. Someone would have to clean it up. It was his mess. No one should have to clean up after him. He should take it even though he'd never wanted it in the first place.

"Leave it," Hayato said.

Masuo hesitated but then crossed his arms, getting into character, and left the bottle. He turned up his nose at every amenity the apartment manager rattled off.

She stopped in front of an elevator. "The model is on the sixth floor, but the available unit is on the tenth."

Masuo gulped.

Arashi had been right. Masuo needed to get over the whole elevator thing, and now would be a perfect time. He didn't want to look like a wimp in front of Hayato.

Smug guy unimpressed by everything in a luxury apartment wouldn't care about riding in a silly elevator. He would step in and be fine. He wouldn't think about what kind of earthquake technology the building used, or how dark it would be if the power went out, or how the elevator could be faulty and he was stepping into a steel coffin of death.

The doors pinged opened, and Masuo jumped.

The manager stepped inside, followed by Hayato.

Masuo's mouth dried, his heart pounded in his ears, and any attempts to stay in character vanished.

He could do it.

He could go into an elevator.

Masuo willed his feet to move, but his muscles clenched down like a vise. Everything within him screamed no.

12

Hayato waited for Masuo to step into the elevator, but he looked like a coat hanger ready to hang in the closet. Then his face turned ashen, and his eyes shut tight. Hayato understood coming face-to-face with an irrational fear. After all, he'd brought Masuo along so he wouldn't be alone.

"You're right, Masuo." Hayato stepped out of the elevator. "The best way to judge a new place is to see how they maintain the stairway. Where are the stairs?"

Masuo let out a shaky laugh. His sandy-brown eyes spoke a volume of thanks. Hayato pushed down the urge to embrace the other man and say everything would be okay.

The manager said, "The stairs are this way."

She escorted them to the end of the hall. Her high heels echoed in the empty, cavernous tower. Hayato climbed the first few steps, then looked back to Masuo. He clutched onto the railing, veins popping out on his hand. He made it up one step, but it would take hours to get to the model at Masuo's current rate.

"We'll meet you up there," Hayato said to the manager.

Concern flooded the woman's face, but Hayato flashed her a smile, and she seemed reassured enough to leave them alone.

"You didn't have to do that." Masuo climbed the next step.

"Her heels were bugging me."

Hayato allowed Masuo to set the pace, slow but steady. One hand gripped the railing while the other stayed stiff at his side. Hayato reached out and interlaced their fingers. Masuo's calloused hands tightened in surprise but then relaxed. An easy warmth washed over Hayato.

Jiro had refused to hold hands anywhere outside the privacy of their home, but Masuo didn't even flinch. Not to mention how considerate he had tried to be when it came to taking a complimentary drink. Hayato had fun with him and envisioned a real date would be more than pleasurable. Masuo would no doubt want to go someplace quaint like an aquarium. They could stay out all night and—

Hayato bit his tongue.

He had to stop diving headfirst into relationships so he didn't have to be alone. He'd done it with Jiro, and that had ended in disaster. Hayato needed to focus on finding his own place and making it alone, for his brother's sake if nothing else.

Drinking with Masuo was fun. The phone sex was fun. Hayato would keep their friendship fun and nothing more. The last thing he wanted was to fall for a guy who wanted marriage and kids.

"Your ring is kind of digging into my finger," Masuo said.

"Oh, sorry." Hayato let go and twisted the amethyst ring back into place.

Masuo clasped their hands together again. "It's pretty."

The marquise-cut stone sat on a silver ring next to two small diamonds. It was his mother's ring. Hayato had been wearing it for years. When it had caught Jiro's attention, he'd always commented on it being too feminine for any man to wear.

Hayato cleared his throat. "So what's your go-to guilty pleasure?"

Masuo hesitated, then a smile spread across his face. "Going to the pet store and getting a cat toy for Mochi. When I get home, she's always so excited and headbutts me as she plays with it. Then five minutes later, she's bored and goes back to sleeping on my shoes. But for those five minutes, she thinks I'm the best cat dad in the world."

"Cat dad?" Hayato laughed. "I'll start calling you that."

"She followed me home one summer night. I opened my door, and she padded inside like it was home."

"She sounds cute."

"I've got photos to prove it."

Masuo let go of the railing and fished out his phone. A whole folder had been dedicated to pictures of the sturdy gray tabby.

"She's cute," Hayato said. "She does look like a puffy

ball of New Year's mochi, especially when she sleeps on your shoes."

"I like to think the hair she leaves inside is her way of making sure I remember her."

"We never had any pets growing up. Dad was allergic to everything."

"Not even a fish?" Masuo asked.

"Especially fish. He said he was allergic to the tank water." Hayato sighed. "Looking back, he'd of course been lying, but I get it. We'd go on long trips at least once a year. It would've been a pain."

"My mom loves cats. We always had at least two or three at home. So what's your guilty pleasure?"

Hayato couldn't say drinking so much he couldn't remember it the next day. He only let himself get that carried away in January. He needed something wholesome.

"I like going to a manga café," Hayato said.

"Fun. I haven't had time to read any outside of *Detective Pom Pom* in years."

"*Detective Pom Pom*?" Hayato hummed a few bars of the theme song. "I loved that show growing up."

Masuo sung the words of the theme, and Hayato laughed, joining in on the words he recalled.

"It's still on," Masuo said. "But they changed the theme song and use 3D graphics now."

"Double boo. The theme song was the best part."

They arrived at the sixth floor, where the apartment manager had waited for them. She looked at their joined hands, but Hayato didn't care. If he was going to live there, management needed to be okay with a flaming gay. She cleared her throat, and Masuo let go.

She led them out of the stairwell and into the staged apartment. She raddled through the amenities—heated wooden floors, large bathtub, double-door closets.

"I don't know." Masuo crossed his arms. "This is far from...ahh...bowling."

"Bowling?" The manager lifted a penciled brow. "That's a first for me. Most of the residents are big golfers, but I'm sure there are a few bowlers as well."

"Good to know. I'm a huge bowler." Hayato mimicked throwing a ball down the alley. "I average almost three hundred each game."

"Such skill," the manager said.

"I don't know if it's worth it to be so far from your usual bowling alley, and these closets..." Masuo huffed. "I think the other place had bigger ones, right?"

Hayato nodded. "That's right. I don't think it will hold all my balls."

The manager opened the entry hall closet. "This offers plenty of storage."

Masuo rolled his eyes. "You clearly haven't seen this man's balls."

Hayato stifled a laugh to keep up the act. "I love playing with so many different balls. Each one has a different feel in the hand, you know? I keep at least a dozen hanging around."

The manager continued to try to win Masuo over, and Hayato made his way to the glass balcony door. He couldn't hear the street below or any neighbors. If the apartment manager and Masuo weren't here, Hayato would be completely alone. People alone made stupid decisions...

The floors and the way the joints lined up in the

transition between the kitchen and the living room resembled the ones in his childhood home. He and Subaru would always line up train tracks throughout the living room and kitchen when they'd played.

Then the horror-filled memory invaded. Hayato's throat grew tight, and each of his attempts to gulp down a breath was in vain. Hayato could see a puddle of urine on the floor. Long gone were the happy train tracks. Subaru had covered his eyes and shoved him out that day. Yet once the police came, they'd left the door wide open. Hayato had seen—

Masuo squeezed Hayato's shoulder, pulling him out of the nightmare. Masuo stood so close his vanilla-and-oak scent wrapped around them, causing the simple squeeze to feel like a full embrace. How could Masuo, who'd known him less than a week, read Hayato better than Jiro?

"You okay?" Masuo kept his voice low.

Hayato gave a little nod.

"What do you think?" the manager asked Hayato.

"It looks nice," Hayato said, surprised his voice came out so steady. He had Masuo to thank for that. "But I think I'd enjoy a place with a little more life to it."

"Our resident lounge is very active. We even have a book club that meets there every week."

Hayato was sure a book club wouldn't want to read the books he'd be interested in, but if it meant meeting some more people...

"Maybe if you show us?" Masuo asked.

"There is a TV and a DVD player for movies," she said.

Masuo shook his head and looked at Hayato with such gentle eyes. "That other place we saw had a theater."

Hayato hid his laugh. Masuo couldn't lie well, and if there wasn't a commission on the line, the manager would've probably noticed.

Hayato shrugged. "Might as well see it."

The manager led them out and down the stairs. Hayato held Masuo's hand on the way down. Somehow it felt a little different. Hayato wasn't only holding it to make Masuo feel calm but because it helped calm him too. Hayato decided not to dwell on it. January shook his feelings around more than a cocktail. He'd probably get the same warm, fuzzy feeling about a pet fish if it meant he wasn't alone.

The manager took them past a door marked Residents Only. Talking erupted from people in every corner. A group stood by the pool table, most of the machines in the gym area were occupied, even the quiet reading nook had someone staring at their phone. Hayato would never be alone again.

He found a place he could live. He could move out of his brother's apartment without the fear of a night alone, and Subaru could finally begin his life with Fumiko. Everything was perfect.

"Eh, it's okay." Masuo failed to look impressed.

Hayato could've sign the leasing papers right then, but with the way Masuo had acted about the complimentary drinks, he'd drop dead when he saw the price. The last thing Hayato needed was another dead pachinko parlor manager.

"We'll think about it," Hayato said.

The manager handed Hayato a glossy folder with

information. Hayato said a friendly goodbye, and he and Masuo left the complex.

"That was fun," Masuo said. "Maybe I should have kept the water bottle as a souvenir. Well, I guess I'll see you."

A sting pinched Hayato's heart. Masuo was going to leave and do his own thing for the rest of the day.

"Do you want to get a drink?" Hayato asked. "I've got a few hours before I have to start making the rounds."

"Sure. Coffee sounds good."

Hayato was thinking about something stronger than coffee, but Masuo wanted coffee, and Hayato wanted to spend time with him.

"There's bound to be a nice café somewhere close by," Hayato said.

"Hopefully one where a coffee doesn't cost half my rent," Masuo said on a laugh.

13

A fter a week, Masuo had settled into the rhythm of being a pachinko manager. The noise of the machines no longer hurt his ears, and he even enjoyed cleaning out the ashtrays and vacuuming after closing.

More and more people flocked to the parlor each day. With the plan he'd cooked up, he'd be raking in the cash. Then he could go all out for the grand reopening in two weeks.

Masuo closed the parlor's gate and went back inside to finish designing the ads he'd bought. Hopefully they would pay off.

He plopped into the creaky office chair and jiggled the old computer's mouse. The ads were important, but so was the atmosphere once the customers arrived. Pachinko machines topped the atmosphere list followed by paint, or maybe paint should be considered third, since bodily fluids stained the carpet? Maybe the store had something cheap they could sell him, but would it last long enough to be worth the price if he had to redo it in a year?

Someone banged on the front gate, and Masuo's phone buzzed. He snatched his phone out of his pocket.

Hayato.

Shit. Masuo must've screwed up big time. He answered his phone and headed to the front. "Whatever I did, I'll fix it."

"Where are you?" Hayato asked.

Masuo opened the gate. "I'm in the parlor."

Hayato stood beside the faded *Lupin*. His honey-colored contacts, usually twinkling and sweet, now held panic. Something must've happened. Masuo's limbs went numb.

"Did the Korean mafia attack?" Masuo asked, putting to words what every Kyoto yakuza feared.

Hayato cleared his throat and tugged up the fuzzy collar of his coat. "What's Subaru doing?"

The air returned to Masuo's lungs, then a wave of angry heat washed over him. "I don't know."

"I'm your boss. You have to tell me the truth even if Subaru made you promise not to tell me."

"I don't know what you're talking about."

Hayato took a step closer, and the scent of his white-flower-and-black-currant perfume followed. Yet no matter how alluring Hayato smelled, his eyes were locked on Masuo like he was prey. No one made it to yakuza captain if they couldn't gut an enemy in seconds, and with that look, any doubt Masuo had about Hayato's ability vanished.

"What happened?" Masuo asked.

Hayato frowned. "He left."

"Your brother left?"

Hayato nodded, the intensity of his gaze softened. He hadn't been ready to fight, but he'd been brought to the edge of fright and ready to lash out in a final attempt to escape.

"When did you last see him?" Masuo asked.

"This evening. When I gave him the code to my new apartment, he told me he was staying at his girlfriend's. I don't care if he told you to keep the housewarming party a secret. I want to know what he said."

Masuo fought his laughter because clearly, to Hayato, a surprise party was a very serious matter.

"I only found out you were moving when you told me earlier today," Masuo said.

"So Subaru didn't call you?"

"You can check my phone if you don't believe me."

Hayato sighed and leaned against the gate. "It's fine. I can tell when you lie, and you're not."

"Why do you think he'd call me?"

"You're in the friend section in my phone."

Masuo's mouth probably hung open a little too long before he realized and closed it. Hayato thought they were friends? He'd said they were at the bar, but Masuo had figured he'd said that to make things easy. Masuo stood up a little straighter and flashed a smile, hoping it read as cool and collected.

"And Subaru's staying the night at his girlfriend's place," Hayato repeated. "He must be doing it so he can pull something off."

"Or maybe he wants to spend the night with her?"

"He wouldn't."

Masuo bit back another laugh. Hayato was serious,

and it wouldn't make him feel any better if Masuo laughed in his face. Though, it did boost Masuo's pride to know when frightened, Hayato came to him. Masuo didn't believe for one second that the housewarming party was the real reason Hayato was there.

"Then maybe Subaru's helping his girlfriend pack." Masuo played along. "You said she was moving in on Friday."

"I know him. He wouldn't leave me alone unless he was planning something."

Hayato rubbed his arms and let out a long sigh. It hung in the cold air a few seconds before evaporating.

"What are you up to?" Hayato shuffled his feet. "Are you heading home?"

"I'm working on some grand reopening strategies."

"I can help."

Bingo. Hayato wanted an excuse to see him, and inventing a surprise party plot had been the excuse he'd needed.

"You don't have to."

Hayato shrugged. "What else am I going to do?"

He could've done a ton of other things, but Masuo thanked him, and they shuffled into the parlor together. Hayato needed him, and Masuo wasn't going to turn him away.

"What's this about?" Hayato pointed to the plastic tubs of pachinko balls stacked on the office floor.

"I had this awesome idea!" Masuo said. "I got together with a dance club manager, and they're handing out coupons to get twenty balls free tomorrow to anyone who attends tonight. All I had to do was put in some drink tickets as prizes, and Friday I have to hang a poster about their disco night. Hopefully it results in more customers tomorrow."

Hayato nodded. "Not bad."

"Really?"

"Maybe you are a real manager after all."

Hayato followed the narrow path between the tubs to the office sofa and lay down, one leg dangling off the side and the other resting on top. The man knew how to make everything a suggestion of sex. If they ever screwed on the sofa, Masuo would never be able to do any work in the room again.

Masuo sat in the desk chair. "What color do you think I should get for the walls?"

"You still haven't decided? Get red. It'll help people feel more energized."

"Red requires primer and, like, two coats of paint."

Hayato shrugged. "So."

"It's expensive," Masuo said.

"Then get a different color."

"But you said red was good. I can get it, but I'll have to budget more for it. If it's too much, then I can't replace the carpet."

"Then get blue. Maybe it will turn everyone into pachinko-playing zombies."

Masuo went back to his grand reopening spreadsheet. Maybe he could splurge on red paint if he put some of his own money into the remodel. He could pay himself once the profits bumped up his salary.

Maybe the paint companies had better suggestions...

Nearly an hour passed before Masuo noticed how much time had slipped by. Masuo tapped his pen against his notepad. What was he doing? He had time alone with Hayato, and he was asking his opinion on paint colors.

Hayato looked bored—beyond sexy, sure, but bored.

Masuo cleared his throat. "Sorry. I'm a bad host. I got into color behavior studies and lost track of time."

"It's nice seeing a manager who takes everything so seriously." Hayato stretched. His shirt rose, showing a sliver of stomach. "The others have their parlors tricked out, so all they do is change the payouts when the computer tells them."

"Have you finished packing?" Masuo asked, moving away from discussions of work. "I can help if you have any last-minute things."

"You already packed all my stuff when you got it from my ex."

"Do you want to go out?"

Hayato suggestively ran his tongue over his bottom lip. "I can think of a lot of fun things we can do together."

Masuo swallowed his desire. "Let's do something different."

Jumping into bed again wouldn't create a new story for their relationship. They were little more than friends who fucked once and continued to cocktease each other with flirting. Masuo wanted something more than sex with Hayato. They couldn't play another round of love hotel fantasy night.

Hayato cocked his head. "Different like what? I don't like screwing in the park when it's cold outside."

"I was thinking about getting a new piercing," Masuo said. "Wanna get one too?"

"Me?"

"You'd look extra hot with one. Maybe we can get matching ones."

Hayato tapped his fingers on the sofa. "Only if I get to pick where they go."

"Deal."

———

A MURAL OF a skull with a snake coming out of the eye sockets greeted Masuo and Hayato before the tattoo and piercing shop assistant could, but she popped out from the back a second later and checked them in. A few customers were ahead of them, so they waited on an ornately carved bench.

Masuo flipped through the portfolio of the woman who was going to pierce them. She did impressive work, and Masuo had heard good things about her.

"You ever thought of getting a piercing before?" Masuo asked.

"They looked like they'd hurt too much." Hayato turned the page and cringed at the photo of a nipple piercing.

"Probably not as much as the huge dragon tattoo on your back."

"That's different."

Masuo laughed. "Where should we get them? I think a sexy place would be nice."

"Sexy places sound the most painful." Hayato pointed to the nipple picture. "It hurts looking at it, and wouldn't people see it through your shirt?"

"That's what makes it sexy."

Hayato pulled out his rose-colored lip gloss and

dabbed it on his lips. "I'd rather never wear lip gloss again than get my nipples pierced."

"What about a magic cross, then?"

"I don't even know what that is, and I can already tell you the answer is no."

"But I hear they make certain activities feel extra good, especially for the partner." Masuo winked.

"And it would probably take months to heal. Imagine if it got infected." Hayato shivered. "No, thank you."

"Well, I think even an ear piercing would be sexy. It naturally draws attention to your neck."

"But people will see it."

Masuo narrowed his eyes. "You don't want people to see it?"

"That's why my tattoo is on my back. And people can't rip it out during a fight."

Masuo had never pegged Hayato, someone who wore makeup, as conservative enough not to want to show off an ear piercing, though maybe it had more to do with his latter point. Clearly, he still had a lot to learn about Hayato, but Masuo was ready for every exciting moment of it.

Hayato took the books and flipped back to the beginning. He stopped at the navel piercings.

"These don't look too bad." Hayato tapped the picture.

Masuo grinned. "So you are going with a sexy location."

Hayato playfully shoved him, but he hadn't expected it and fell off the bench. They both burst into laughter.

"You two aren't wasted, are you?" the receptionist asked.

"No, I'm just really gay." Hayato held up his hand.

It didn't take much longer for their turn to come, probably because the shop employees didn't want more hysterical laughter coming from the waiting area.

Their piercer was a short woman with a panther tattooed on her arm. Ironically, while the mob suggested new recruits skip tattoos, they were getting more popular with the general public. Masuo liked them, since it automatically made it easier to identify people with an open mind.

She pulled on her gloves. "Who's going first?"

Masuo offered himself up first in case after seeing it done, Hayato changed his mind.

"Would it be easier if I take off my shirt?" he asked.

Hayato rolled his eyes. "Don't listen to him. He's trying to impress me."

She laughed and had Masuo stand and hold up his shirt as she marked where the piercing would be as he stood. He checked it in the mirror and gave his okay, then lay down on the table as the piercer explained the process. Masuo wasn't worried, so he only half listened, choosing to focus on Hayato instead. His eyes were wide, and his head nodded along with whatever the woman said.

"Okay, deep breath and—"

"Wait," Hayato said. "Doesn't he need to hold on to something for the pain or need, like, a stick to bite down on?"

The woman blinked. "It shouldn't—"

"Ah, thanks. You saved me there," Masuo said and held out his hand to Hayato. "You don't mind?"

Hayato cupped his hand around Masuo's. Hayato's

grip was so tight it would probably hurt more than the piercing, but Masuo let him squeeze. It wasn't for him anyway.

"Are we good?" she asked.

"I'm ready now." He smiled at Hayato.

The cleanup took longer than the piercing, and in a few minutes, Masuo had a new hole in his body.

"It's okay if you change your mind," Masuo said.

"No, I want to do it."

Hayato lifted up his shirt. His dark jeans hung so low the top of the scar on his stomach showed. It didn't look more than a few months old. Whatever it was from, it must've hurt.

The woman explained all the steps like she'd done with Masuo, perhaps going a little slower for Hayato's sake, and he held Masuo's hand from the very start.

Warm fuzzies were an understatement. Holding Hayato's hand was like snuggling under warm blankets on a snowy day when he knew he wouldn't have to leave the house. Like waking up from one night of amazing sex and knowing it was going to turn into something more.

Maybe the latter could still be true.

"Okay, all done," the woman said.

Hayato blinked. "Really?"

"Yup."

"That wasn't bad at all."

"It's because you were holding hands," the woman said, giving Masuo a little nod. "It's the best method to drive back the pain."

Masuo was going to leave the shop the best review ever.

"Thank you. I couldn't have done it without you," Hayato said.

Hayato's eyes sparkled, and Masuo's lips tingled. His heart took over. He leaned over and kissed Hayato. His lips soft and moist. Masuo could've kissed him until the night turned to day, but then his brain kicked in, and he pulled back.

"I'm sorry," Masuo said.

Hayato pulled Masuo back and dominated the kiss. His tongue traced Masuo's lips until they parted, and he dove inside. Masuo's tongue met Hayato's like they were making love and melting into one.

Hayato pulled back this time.

"Never apologize for kissing me." Hayato spoke so sternly Masuo wouldn't dare do it again.

The piercer didn't bat an eye at the display of affection and finished up telling Hayato the finer points of taking care of his sexy new hole.

They left the piercing studio, and Hayato jumped up and down.

"I feel like I could fly," he said. "I can see why you get them done."

"It's a rush, isn't it?"

"Want to go to a love hotel? I feel like I could go all night."

Masuo nibbled on his lip piercing. Everything inside him was screaming yes, but what was stopping it from turning into New Year's all over again? Sure, they weren't drunk, but it felt too fast for the meaningful relationship Masuo wanted. The week they'd spent as friends had been so nice. Would one night of passion be worth spoiling what they were working toward?

"I gotta get to the parlor early tomorrow," Masuo said.

"Set your alarm."

"I think if I end up in bed with you again, I'll never want to leave." Masuo spoke from the heart.

Hayato laughed, and it crushed Masuo.

"And you said you were moving in to your apartment first thing tomorrow morning," Masuo said. "You don't want to miss it, do you?"

Hayato smiled. At least he wasn't laughing.

"Why don't you help me move in?" Hayato asked.

"You mean it?"

Knowing where Hayato lived had to mean he was ready to take their relationship to the next step.

"Get there at eight. You'll have plenty of time before work. I'll text you the address in the morning."

"I'll be there."

Hayato gave him another scorching kiss and pulled back with a wink. "Something to remember me by. See you tomorrow, and you'd better wear something hot. I'll help you change into your work suit when you leave."

Hayato blew into his gloved hands. Even inside the lobby of his new apartment, the bitter January cold found him.

The doors opened, and another chilling breeze followed Masuo inside. Hayato hoped his lip gloss hadn't frozen his mouth shut so he could smile.

"Thanks for helping me move," Hayato said.

Masuo looked around. "When we came here, I thought we were doing it for fun."

"You didn't have fun?"

"I did, but I thought it was for the list."

"We did both at the same time. What's wrong with that?" Hayato hoped the answer satisfied, since he couldn't remember what list Masuo was talking about.

Masuo motioned to the single suitcase. "You barely need my help."

"Still, I wanted to say thanks." Hayato reached into his pocket and pulled out a small wrapped gift.

"You didn't have to get me anything."

"It's not for you. It's for Mochi. You know, as a thanks for letting me take her cat dad in the morning. She likes catnip mice, right?"

"Loves them." Masuo laughed. "I'll be sure to make sure she writes a proper thank-you note."

"That's being a good cat dad."

Hayato hadn't been sure Masuo would like it, since Hayato had thought up the idea at five in the morning.

Last night, after Masuo had rejected Hayato's love hotel invite, he'd accidentally fallen asleep at the manga café, since he wasn't going to spend the night at Subaru's apartment alone. It had showers, and foreigners used it as a cheap hotel all the time, so the staff was used to it, but the uncomfortable beanbag had woken him up too early to move. So he'd sashayed around any random store open. One happened to be a pet store.

"Ready to get going?" Masuo asked. "I can meet you up there."

"Oh, honey, we need to go together or else we'll ruin it for Subaru."

Masuo blinked. "What?"

"I told you yesterday. Subaru's obviously planning some kind of party."

"Or he wanted to spend the night with his girlfriend."

Hayato rolled his eyes. "Sure, maybe that too."

Masuo laughed. "Here. Let me take your bag, since I'm the reason we're taking the stairs."

Hayato allowed Masuo to carry the suitcase. He took off his jacket and rolled up his sleeves to lug the thing up, and while he might not have taken Hayato's suggestion of wearing street clothes, the man did look hot in his suit, especially with the way his muscles contracted around his rolled sleeve. Hayato craved reenacting their New Year's evening so he could remember.

They arrived at the door.

"Now, you gotta act surprised," Hayato said.

"I can do that." Masuo looked at the electronic panel on the door. "Wait, this place is so fancy they don't have keys?"

"It's another excuse to charge more in rent."

Hayato typed in the apartment code. The device made a happy chime, and they entered. The large windows made it impossible to hide in the dark, but Fumiko and Subaru still jumped out.

"Surprise!" they cheered.

Hayato faked surprise, and Masuo mustered up a better act than the last time they'd been at the apartment. Subaru held up a small cake with glazed fruit and Welcome Home written in the center. Fumiko held up the real treat, a cocktail glass. The drink was bright red, which matched the cherries on her dress.

"How long have you two been planning this?" Hayato asked. "I had no idea."

"My little brother's first home all by himself? Of course I had to make it special," Subaru said.

Hayato playfully punched Subaru's arm. "Thanks."

"I even came up with a new cocktail." Fumiko handed Hayato and Masuo each a glass.

"Yes, please."

Subaru had ended up buying real dishes and silverware. He must've thought Hayato wouldn't be responsible enough to buy them himself. It was probably true. Takeout seemed so much easier than dealing with dishes.

Hayato introduced Masuo to everyone, and Subaru sliced up the cake. They sat on the floor, since there weren't any chairs.

"I can't believe you actually moved here. This place looks so expensive," Masuo said.

Hayato shook his head. "We got a nice bump in salary after the war or else this wouldn't be anywhere near my budget."

Fumiko passed another cake slice to Masuo. "I can't wait to see how you'll decorate it."

"I don't even know where to start."

Subaru grinned. "Start with a table. That way, we don't have to hold our plates when you invite us over for dinner next week."

He'd clearly already made plans, probably so he could still keep an eye on him.

Moving in hadn't fully sunken in for Hayato. What did it mean to live alone? Coming home to an empty apartment. No one there to greet him. Knowing no one, ready to tell Hayato about his day. Hayato would have to enjoy his solitude, but the thought turned his breathing shallow.

He pushed the looming thoughts aside. If Subaru could start the next phase of his life, Hayato could start his by getting over his monophobia.

Hayato asked Fumiko about the next dance competition. When she got going about swing dancing, she could go on and on. Since Masuo knew nothing, they could avoid talking about the apartment and all the new responsibilities Hayato had to deal with.

With the last slice of cake finished, Hayato put his plate in the sink. Only an hour into owning his own place and he already had dirty dishes. Subaru walked over while Fumiko explained some of the finer points of swing to Masuo.

"You going to be okay?" Subaru asked.

"I'll be fine." What else could Hayato say?

"Some days might feel darker than others. I'm always only a phone call away no matter what time it is."

Hayato smiled, but it felt fake. "Don't worry about me. You keep your focus on defending your title at the next hop, or Fumiko might dump you for a stronger partner."

She strolled over with a big grin. "He's not wrong, you know."

"Got it, got it. I'll keep my eye on the prize." Subaru held up his hands.

"Honey cake, why don't we give Hayato and Masuo some alone time." Fumiko winked at Hayato.

He'd known he liked her for a reason.

Subaru gave Hayato one of his proud big-brother hugs that wasn't really necessary, since Hayato's apartment was a ten-minute bus ride away from Subaru's. Hayato didn't deserve him sometimes. Other times they were even on the awesome brother scale, but in January, Subaru always won.

They gave a friendly goodbye to Masuo and left.

Hayato stretched out his arms. "Freedom."

"Your brother's nice," Masuo said.

"Only when he's not trying to win the most serious person in the world award."

"You'll have to take up bowling now."

"Oh yes. I'll start a team with my neighbors."

Hayato made another set of cocktails using Fumiko's recipe and the alcohol she'd gifted him. Talk about the best housewarming present ever. He handed Masuo's glass back to him. He didn't drink any, but that didn't stop Hayato from taking a few big sips of his.

Hayato pulled Masuo close and planted a full kiss on his sweet lips. Hayato dove one of his hands beneath Masuo's shirt. His soft skin covered a set of hard abs.

Hayato dropped his hand from Masuo's cheek to the back of his neck and guided them down to the heated wooden floors. The kiss was deep, long, and lustful. Hayato put everything he could into it, making sure Masuo understood what he craved.

Hayato opened his legs a little wider, all but begging Masuo to fuck him into next month. But Masuo pulled back and sat on his haunches. His brow wrinkled worse than a condom forgotten in a wallet. He was going to say something, wasn't he?

"I..." Masuo bit at his lip ring.

Hayato put a reassuring hand on Masuo's thigh that could easily be moved into a more suggestive location should the mood get back to hot and heavy.

"What is it?" Hayato asked. "You can tell me."

"I really like you," Masuo said.

"I like you too."

"Then can we be boyfriends?"

Hayato's eyes went wide.

He couldn't dive headfirst into another relationship and be stuck living with a man who refused to bring handcuffs into the bedroom. But Hayato had moved into a place by himself. It was the biggest step he had ever taken to conquer his monophobia. He wouldn't be diving in headfirst if he lived by himself.

"I just..." Masuo swallowed, his Adam's apple

bobbing. "I'm not a friends-with-benefits kind of guy. If that's you, cool, but I need to know where we stand in our relationship."

Masuo was being clingy again. Though, if they dated, it didn't mean Masuo had to be Hayato's last boyfriend. With his own place to call home, Hayato didn't need to rely on a boyfriend as much as before. Nothing was stopping him from dating Masuo and seeing how it went. If it didn't work, they could break up.

Hayato shrugged. "Sure, we can be boyfriends."

Masuo's sandy-colored eyes glowed like the bottom of a bourbon bottle. "You mean it?"

"Yeah. Did you think I would turn you down?"

"I mean..." Masuo rubbed his neck.

"Come on, even I have to admit you were right." Hayato's hand moved closer to Masuo's crotch. "We have great chemistry."

Not to mention Masuo had a massive cock that Hayato was ready to see in action.

Masuo pressed his lips together. "Then I should probably tell you you're actually the first guy I've been with."

No wonder Masuo had become so clingy so fast.

"It's no big deal. Everyone has to have a first sometime. Mine was at fourteen. Yours was twenty-three?" Hayato guessed Masuo's age.

"Twenty."

Damn. They were ten years apart. No wonder Masuo had barely any refractory time. All the better to relive their New Year's tryst.

Hayato smiled, his hand on Masuo's inner thigh, his fingertips lightly teasing Masuo's crotch. The heat of his inner thigh warmed Hayato's hand, and the whiff of sugary cherry liquor from Masuo's drink only pushed Hayato to want to show Masuo a good time.

"I need to get going. The parlor opens soon." Masuo cupped his hand over Hayato's, preventing him from moving it any farther.

"I'm your boss. I give you permission to be late."

"But I made a deal with the club upstairs. People are probably waiting."

Masuo was such a workaholic, but if his plan worked, it would make his parlor a lot of money. If word got back to Endo that Hayato had botched Masuo's brilliant marketing strategy to get some dick, Hayato would never get back into her good graces.

Hayato leaned back. "You'd better make so much money I have to buy another briefcase."

"I wish."

"You can do it, honey cake."

Masuo laughed. "I'm not much for honey cake."

"Hmm...I'll come up with something better, sugarplum."

"No food."

Hayato smiled. "Got it, sweet lips."

"Okay, then, diamond sugar."

"We'll have to work on the pet names." Hayato wrapped his arms around Masuo and pressed their foreheads together.

Masuo made sure their kiss was brief. He gave a cheerful goodbye and left.

The door shut, and Hayato hung his head. He might as well get to unpacking while he was riding the make-out high.

He rolled his suitcase into the bedroom, hung his clothes, and lined up all his makeup along the bedroom floor. Even though he'd taken the time to arrange everything from the lightest shade of pink to the darkest, the whole thing had taken under an hour. He didn't need to go to work for another seven.

Hayato clicked off the lights and went back into the living room. The sun shined through the living room windows like it had in his childhood home. Exactly like that day his mother... He grew cold and swallowed hard. He could see her shadow on the wooden floor and the pool of urine. A whiff of decay lingered in the stale air.

He was alone.

No one would be there to stop him from ending it all.

He fled, running down the hall and only slowing when he got to the elevator. He smashed the button to take him to the ground floor and headed straight into the lounge.

People surrounded him, and he felt like he'd come up for air after diving too deep into the sea. He couldn't do anything stupid with other people around.

A large group crowded around the pool table.

"Hey, can I join the next round?" Hayato squeezed into the group. "I'm Hayato. I just moved in today."

They welcomed him, and Hayato wasn't alone.

15

A week after officially becoming Masuo's boyfriend, Hayato was ready to rank their relationship among his top ten. They didn't argue. Masuo was kindhearted, albeit a workaholic but not enough to avoid a late-night movie when Hayato suggested one. Really, he had no complaints.

Except the few times their nightly movie make-out sessions had left Hayato hot and wanting. He'd suggest going to a love hotel close by. Sure, it would be two in the morning, and Hayato expected the three-condom standard Masuo had set before. So what if they'd finish at five and Masuo had to go to work a few hours after? No matter how sweet the fantasy played out in Hayato's mind, Masuo always rejected the offer.

If it wasn't for his blue balls, Hayato would rank their relationship in his top five.

With Masuo's grand reopening a week away, Hayato would probably have to wait until then to finally get down and dirty. Maybe it was a bit selfish. It was his own fault for not remembering their New Year's sex extravaganza.

Today, Hayato wasn't going to meet Masuo after work, since he'd be painting. Nothing sounded more boring than watching paint dry.

Hayato strolled into his apartment lobby and headed for the resident lounge.

"Mr. Kobayashi," the manager called.

She came out from the office hallway like she'd been waiting there all night. Her long hair had been tied back in a tight ponytail.

"Yes?" Hayato said. "I love the new apartment. Thanks again for your help with all the paperwork."

"Would you come with me to my office? There's something we need to talk about." The woman's serious tone set Hayato on edge.

Hopefully it wasn't the yakuza talk. He'd always figured he acted gay enough no one would believe he was a mobster. One of the late-night billiards players might've seen Hayato's tattoo and complained. Tattoos weren't illegal, but they sure carried a stigma and made people jump to conclusions. All Hayato had to do was calm the manager down and swear he hadn't drunk sake with the Kyoto godfather.

Hayato followed the manager to her office and got ready to fake shock at the accusation of being called one of the big, bad, scary yakuza.

She sat behind her large wooden desk, and her expression soured. The air grew thicker than when Hayato had been in high school and his counselor had asked him why he wasn't applying himself like he'd done the years before.

"Did I forget to put my seal on one of the leasing pages?" he asked.

"We're glad you enjoy all the amenities we have to offer," she said.

"I've met so many neighbors at the lounge. We're becoming good friends."

"That's good. Maybe invite them to your apartment. You see, we've been getting some complaints."

Hayato's eyes narrowed. "Complaints?"

"You've been found sleeping in the lounge on several occasions."

"I start a movie and accidentally fall asleep. Who hasn't done that?"

She frowned. "It's making some residents uncomfortable."

"Oh." An empty feeling erupted inside Hayato's gut like a sinkhole swallowing a street.

"People are saying that every time they come into the lounge, you're there, trying to make conversation even if they want to be left alone," she continued as if talking to a child.

Hayato crossed his arms, his cheeks burning. He couldn't explain to the manager how being alone made him envision his slow, painful death until it brought him to tears. How his throat would close and leave him gasping for breath.

"I'm excited to meet everyone." Hayato hoped his voice sounded more confident than he felt.

"We take every complaint seriously, and we've had several already. We are being generous and putting you on strike two. I'm afraid if we get one more, we'll have to ask you to leave."

"You can't kick me out. I signed the lease last week. My rent pays for those amenities. It's like people have never seen someone sleeping before. Salarymen sleep on the subway all the time, and no one cares."

She pulled out Hayato's leasing agreement and pointed to a highlighted section on the page. "You see here, it clearly states—"

Hayato stood. "Whatever."

"Mr. Kobayashi—"

"I get it! I won't hang out in the lounge anymore."

He stormed out and smashed the elevator button, trying to quell his anger as the car ascended to his floor. His frustration had mostly subsided, then he reached his door. A paper had been taped to it. The word *creep* had been written in thick, blocky letters that took up the whole sheet. He ripped it off, crumpled it up, and left it on the floor.

The door slammed shut behind him, and he changed out of his suit and into street clothes. He was so frustrated the solitude didn't sink in until he went into the living room.

Still empty.

Even the futon he'd bought had remained in plastic wrap, since he hadn't slept in the apartment. He needed to buy furniture. He had managed to convince Subaru to host their weekly dinner at his place, but that would only buy Hayato so much time to pretend he had his life together.

What even was his style?

His ex was into modern stuff, which had never appealed to Hayato. When he'd lived with Subaru, they'd gotten whatever junk was cheapest.

As a child, their mother had decorated their house in a California-beach style to relive her exchange student days.

Hayato laughed, imagining the same bright-yellow surfboard coffee table in the center of his empty living room. He bit his lip as the memory turned painful.

It had really happened. Twenty years ago. It felt so far away until Hayato closed his eyes. Then he was ten again, walking home from school. Their father had left the night before on a three-week business trip, and they were alone with their mom.

Dad had put Subaru in charge and given him a large envelope of cash to pay for everything down to the rent. Mom had been sick all year. She'd turned into a completely different person. They'd have to take care of her and the household chores.

When Dad had left for his trip, the little light in her eyes had faded. No wonder she'd...

Hayato swallowed, not daring to think the words, too afraid of evoking the vision. His fingers went numb, and a cold chill shook him to his marrow. He couldn't stay here alone. His thoughts would drift, and within minutes, he probably wouldn't be able to control them.

No one would be here to stop him.

It got hard to breathe.

He grabbed his coat and left. Watching paint dry with Masuo suddenly sounded a lot more interesting.

THE PAINT FUMES hit Hayato before he got near the parlor. Masuo stood on a ladder, stripped down to his white undershirt and completely absorbed in painting. He sighed, grabbing the end of his shirt and using it to dab a bit of sweat off his brow. The man had such delicious abs.

"Hey, sexy. You missed a spot," Hayato said.

Masuo looked down with the biggest smile on his face. It almost made Hayato forget how horrible January was.

"You changed your mind about coming," Masuo said.

"Well, you know." Hayato held up one of the hot-chocolate drinks he'd picked up along the way. "Happy one-week anniversary. Or do you want to call it two? We'd have a better first date story about hot New Year's sex if we say two weeks. I do kind of feel bad I don't remember it, but that means I can make up more outlandish things if anyone asks what we did."

Masuo ignored the offered cup and climbed down the ladder to embrace Hayato. He could've been outside on the chilliest day for hours and the way Masuo hugged him would've warmed him. In his embrace, all the horrible things with the apartment and the crappy month grew to distant memories.

"Thank you." Masuo squeezed a little tighter. "I was thinking about saying it was our one-week anniversary, but I thought you might think it was sappy."

"Oh, honey, come on. We're together now. Nothing is too sappy, but I can think of a lot more ways we can celebrate than with some hot chocolate."

Masuo pulled Hayato closer by his waist and kissed him. Hayato let out a little gasp of surprise, and Masuo took the upper hand to deepen the kiss. His hands cupped Hayato's face. It wasn't sloppy or sexy like Hayato would've said he wanted, but it was everything he needed.

Masuo pulled back, his smile lighting up the room. A calm flooded Hayato's body. He almost didn't mind the parting because he'd been so satisfied.

"I'm happy you came," Masuo said. "I've been enjoying our late-night outings."

"I have too."

"I would like to keep kissing you, but I have to get this coat finished." Masuo picked up his paint roller.

"You went with white paint?" Hayato asked.

"This is the primer."

"It's streaky over there."

"It's the primer." Masuo said it like Hayato was supposed to know what that meant.

The minutes passed.

Hayato sighed and rocked side to side on one of the pachinko stools. Watching paint dry wasn't the most riveting date.

"Arashi gave me a contact for used machines," Masuo said after ten minutes of silent painting. "Have you heard of a guy called Tall Ken?"

"I wouldn't want to go drinking with him, but sure."

"He says he's got a few of the new *Castle Vampire* machines, but they're not supposed to be officially released for a few months. Is it legit?"

"He's got some connections."

"So I should trust him?"

Hayato finished the last of his hot chocolate. "I should probably go with you. He owes me a favor, and I can make sure he gives you a good price."

"Monday night?" Masuo stepped down from the

ladder, moved it a little bit, and climbed back to move to the next section of wall.

"It's a date. A boring date but a date."

"I'll make it up to you."

Hayato's arm snaked around Masuo's waist. His usual oak-and-vanilla scent was mixed with a deep musk from all the work he'd been doing. Hayato's fingers crawled up Masuo's delicious abs.

"You'll make it up to me tonight?" Hayato whispered into Masuo's ear and gave it a soft nibble.

"I need to finish this coat tonight."

Hayato groaned.

"I promise I'll make it up to you."

Hayato grabbed Masuo's neglected hot chocolate and took a sip. "Fine."

Masuo finished the next section of wall before climbing down the ladder and doing it all over again.

"How about a movie?" Hayato asked.

"When?" Masuo said.

"Next week? The twenty-second. Since you're being such a workaholic until the opening."

"But that's the day of the opening."

"What better way to celebrate?" Hayato said.

Masuo shook his head. "I think I'll be too tired."

"The day before, then?"

"Then I'll be busy preparing for the opening."

Hayato let out a dramatic sigh. "You're getting way too good at this job."

"I promise we can see a movie the day after."

But Hayato didn't need the distraction on the twenty-third as much as the day before.

Hayato poked around on his phone until Masuo finished a half hour later.

"All done," Masuo said.

"Can I at least buy you a beer to celebrate all your hard work?" Hayato said, knowing his tone sounded as annoyed as he felt. How could he ever accuse Masuo of being clingy after Hayato had hung out with Masuo every day for the past week?

"Okay, one beer," Masuo said. "Let me get changed."

"Can I watch?"

Masuo laughed and shut the office door behind him.

So Hayato waited, but it took forever.

"Did the paint fumes make you so high you forgot how to button your shirt?" Hayato knocked and waited but got no reply.

Hayato opened the office door, his jaw dropped, and a fire lit inside him.

16

"You yakuza are at it again." Masuo tapped a set of handcuffs against his palm. "I'm going to have to take you in."

Masuo doubted he could keep the authoritarian police tone going for long. Dressing the part had helped get him into character, but with the glimmer in Hayato's eyes, Masuo doubted he'd stay dressed for long.

"Oh no, Mr. Police Officer." Hayato pitched his voice high and dramatic. "I can't possibly go to jail."

Anticipation nipped at Masuo's nerves. He'd somehow managed to reject all Hayato's lascivious advances with a mix of fortitude and a nagging doubt Hayato took their relationship as anything other than a love hotel bingo card. But when he'd strolled in with a hot chocolate to celebrate their one-week anniversary, the uncertainty had vanished, and Masuo dug out the police costume he'd stored in the back.

"I suppose you'll have to *convince* me you're innocent," Masuo said.

"I'll do anything." Hayato arched his back against the doorframe.

"Anything?"

"Anything."

Masuo thrust out his hips. "Then you'd better get to thinking what might help me change my mind."

Hayato withdrew his lip gloss from the pocket of his cigarette pants and smoothed on a dusty-rose color. If the applicator had been his cock, Masuo would've come right then.

"Certainly, Mr. Officer," Hayato purred.

He dropped to his knees. White flowers and black currants, the smell of Hayato's skin, enveloped them. The jingle of Masuo's unbuckled belt tolled like a distant bell. Then Hayato buried his face in Masuo's crotch, and all his thoughts flew away like a spring breeze.

In that single moment, Masuo realized he wasn't in charge. Hayato controlled how things played out. He looked up, catching Masuo's gaze, a mischievous glint in his amber eyes. His eyes were a cool stream on a warm spring day. Masuo could strip naked and swim in those amber pools. Masuo wet his lips, hungry for Hayato's expertise.

He pulled down Masuo's zipper with his teeth. His nose dug through the slit in Masuo's boxers. Hayato's warm breath on his cock made Masuo realize how woefully unprepared he was for sober Hayato. He pulled out Masuo's cock, and his eyes grew wide.

"You're pierced," Hayato said with a gasp.

Masuo grinned. "I'm full of surprises."

Not really. The frenum piercing was the only one not visible during his day-to-day. Still, Hayato reverently ran his thumb over the two silver balls resting underneath the head. The stroking was gentle at first like he was brushing the petals of a flower. Masuo moaned, tossing his head back, and Hayato's touches grew more determined, bringing Masuo fully erect.

Then Hayato's shining lips opened.

"Here, let me get a cond—"

Hayato's tongue licked up Masuo's length, paying extra attention to the gauged barbell. He pulled away, nuzzling the cock like a cat with a toy.

"You know, I always expected cops to be a little rougher and dirtier," Hayato said. "Especially when dealing with the likes of a nasty yakuza."

"Oh, is that what you want?" Masuo swallowed back a moan.

"If that's okay, Mr. Officer."

"I'll keep that in mind."

The number of horror stories Masuo had heard of the police breaking yakuza ribs and smashing fingers because cops knew yakuza wouldn't bring up police brutality were staggering. Not to mention all the horrible things they did to foreigners. No doubt Hayato simply meant rough sex and some dirty talk. Masuo swallowed; without the drinks to cut the edge, he'd worried if he'd hold up to Hayato's expectations.

Masuo pulled out of Hayato's touch.

"Then strip and put on a show for me. Or else," Masuo said, the sharp tone in his voice surprising even him.

Masuo sat on the sofa, hand on his cock, already missing Hayato's tongue. Though, the thin line of lingering saliva on the glans caused a shameless moan to echo from his throat.

Hayato unwrapped his scarf in slow, deliberate turns. Then his hips swung to the soft melody he hummed. Masuo drank in the scene before him. He reached down and slowly stroked his cock. Their gazes met, and Hayato's beauty struck Masuo like a summer storm. His body went into shock. His ears roared with the sounds of his beating heart.

The buttons of Hayato's coat came next. He worked them through and shrugged off the garment. He paused and bit his lip in mock nervousness.

"Did I tell you to stop?" Masuo's voice dripped with lust.

"No, Mr. Officer."

"Then keep going!"

Masuo kept the strokes to his dick slow, determined to have Hayato's mouth be the thing to pull him over the edge. The contrast between the cold chill of the office and the heat from each pull and tug caused every exposed piece of skin to prickle.

If Masuo had any doubt about Hayato's enjoyment, it vanished when he saw the bulge in his pants. Masuo could even make out a distinct dark patch where the tip of Hayato's cock sat.

"Is that why you were so hesitant?" Masuo asked.

Hayato looked down, pretending to be bashful. "I love a man in uniform."

"Let's see how much you love them."

Hayato grabbed the ends of his jersey shirt and in a fluid motion pulled it off over his head. For someone who complained about the cold so much, Hayato didn't layer up. Without an undershirt, his skin pebbled in the cold and his dark nipples hardened. They would look amazing pierced. Maybe in a few years. Though the silver barbell through his navel was damn sexy.

Masuo gathered the precum leaking from his cock and slathered it around the head. His tongue grew heavy.

The sound of Hayato's fly unzipping snapped Masuo's attention back to the present. Hayato took his time peeling back his tight pants, exposing more and more skin until they were so low it was obvious he wasn't wearing underwear. Masuo didn't know how Hayato could do it and not freeze his balls off.

He stepped out of his pants shamelessly, cock glistening with precum and looking painfully hard.

"Now, let's see what that mouth of yours can do," Masuo said.

Hayato's Adam's apple bobbed, and he kneeled in front of Masuo, then swallowed him whole. The man had no gag reflex. Masuo bit his lip, keeping himself from spoiling the tough-cop act by moaning, but that didn't stop Hayato. He hummed around Masuo's cock and let each slip and suckle hang in the air like a misty rain.

Masuo's fingers laced in Hayato's bronze hair, guiding him deeper with each of his expert licks that left Masuo shuddering. The heat of Hayato's mouth, the sounds of love in the air, and the musk of ecstasy mixed with the fruity bite of Hayato's perfume filled Masuo's senses.

"I'm gonna—"

Masuo loosened his grasp so Hayato could pull away, but instead he dove deeper. Masuo's hips frantically bucked, making his cock hit the back of Hayato's throat. But Hayato took everything Masuo had to give and then some. He shot his load, and Hayato sucked him dry, tongue lapping at his spent length like a melting ice cream cone. Masuo's dick slid from Hayato's swollen lips, leaving Masuo breathless. He pulled Hayato onto the sofa and into his arms.

Masuo stroked the side of Hayato's cheek before their lips met in a sloppy kiss. He could taste himself on Hayato's lips.

"That piercing is so hot," Hayato said.

"See? I told you piercings can be very erotic."

Hayato purred into Masuo's ear. "You still up for playing Mr. Officer? It's no fun unless both people are enjoying it."

Masuo bit his lip. Had he been so shit at the role-playing Hayato thought he wasn't enjoying himself? Masuo should've waited so he could make a list of all the things he could do in a sexy cop role-play.

Hayato ran his finger along Masuo's forehead. "You're going to get an ugly wrinkle here if you keep on worrying. It's sex. It's supposed to be fun. Go with the flow. Be spontaneous."

"I—"

Hayato grabbed Masuo's hand and placed it on his erect length. "See how hard you've made me? I can't wait to have you balls deep inside me. I want to feel that piercing scrape my walls. I want you to fuck me into next month. Can you do that?"

Hayato's words caused an erotic wave Masuo had never experienced before. He could barely comprehend the finer details, but Hayato's cock was humping his hand, and Masuo understood.

Hayato kissed him again before giving Masuo's soft dick a few pumps.

"You come back fast, right?" he asked.

Masuo nodded.

"I expected as much." Hayato bit his lip, working a light touch from Masuo's sac to his tip. "Little Masuo isn't so little. I know I said I wanted it rough, but give me a little time to adjust. I haven't had anything that big while sober in a long time. That work?"

"I can do it."

"Thanks, Mr. Officer."

Masuo took that as his signal to jump back into the role-play. He sucked and nipped at Hayato's neck until he let out a sweet string of moans. His hard length had been neglected, but it didn't stop Hayato from thrusting his hips toward him, begging to be touched. Begging for release. The rough fabric of Masuo's pants couldn't have felt good, but a cop wouldn't care about Hayato's comfort. Masuo would keep his pants on knowing how glorious the friction of skin and fabric could be.

Maybe a cop wouldn't leave a trail of hickeys on Hayato's skin, but Masuo couldn't help it. He wanted to mark Hayato like a bee sting. A lingering kind of beauty in the nip of pain. Something he'd remember after the night was over.

Masuo left Hayato's nipples and tongued around his belly button.

"This looks good," Masuo said.

Hayato arched his back. "You think it's sexy, Mr. Officer?"

"Very. You walk around all sexy throwing yourself all over me."

"How could I not throw myself at you?"

"I should arrest you for indecent exposure."

"Oh no." Hayato opened his legs wider.

"Now you're asking for it."

"Hmm."

Masuo opened the desk drawer and took out a condom and a mostly empty bottle of lube he'd brought from home. He'd put them there knowing one day he'd finally take Hayato up on his innuendo about filling him up with his load every time he came to collect the day's earnings.

"I need to do a proper search before I take you in," Masuo said.

He slathered his fingers with the lube, and Hayato put himself more on display. One leg stretched to the top of the sofa, while his other leg bent at the knee to lift him up that much more.

Masuo pressed one of his lubed fingers against Hayato's pink bud. Hayato's eyes were half closed. He let out a sweet little moan, and Masuo wanted to hear it every day and then some.

"Look at this. You're swallowing my finger," Masuo teased. "You must be starving."

"I'm hungry for you." Hayato lifted his hips a little more. "Right there, Mr. Officer."

"You like it here?"

Masuo pushed another finger inside and kept pressing the spot that left Hayato writhing. His chest glistened with sweat, and he used his arms to push himself up.

"You're getting off from only my fingers," Masuo said. "Aren't you?"

Masuo knew Hayato was watching, and that fact alone pushed Masuo to accentuate the movements.

Scissor.

Push.

Scissor.

Hayato completely surrendered. His moans were louder than a thunderstorm and left Masuo ready to burst.

"And you're leaking here." Masuo rubbed the head of Hayato's cock.

"Mr. Officer, you seem to be excited again. Is there anything you want me to assist with?"

"I think there's one thing you can help me with."

"Really?"

Masuo grabbed Hayato's leg from the top of the sofa and brought it down. "I think you can figure it out."

He guided Hayato into position, his face pushed down on the sofa's arm while his ass stayed in the air, waiting for more. His tattoo of twin red-and-blue dragons covered his entire back. Another work of art Masuo could admire along with the rest of the lines of Hayato's body.

Masuo rolled on the condom and pressed at Hayato's entrance. His words echoed in Masuo's mind. He took his time, probably going too slow for what Hayato wanted, as his hips kept on rocking back for more, but Masuo kept him in place.

Masuo's thrusts were slow at first, going in a little farther each time. Hayato let out a string of strangled cries, each one somehow louder and hoarser. Then Masuo gave a final rock of his hips.

"I'm all the way in." He nipped at Hayato's back.

"You're so big."

Hayato couldn't have stroked Masuo's ego more than he had in that moment. Hayato pulled forward a bit before pushing back, fucking himself while Masuo was distracted. Masuo took over and set a steady rhythm.

Hayato's nostrils flared. His mouth opened wide on a string of guttural grunts. He pushed back, meeting each of Masuo's thrusts, silently begging him to go deeper, harder, faster!

Hayato was even more delicious than Masuo remembered, and the snap of his hips sent the small sofa rocking.

Hayato's hand snaked down to give himself some relief, but Masuo grabbed Hayato's wrist.

"Who said you could do that?" Masuo said. "I can't trust you yakuza, can I?"

Masuo snatched the handcuffs that had fallen between the cushions, pulled Hayato's hands behind his back, and cuffed them. Hayato let out a frustrated groan. It almost felt a little mean, but Hayato wanted a rough and dirty cop, so he got one.

Hayato's neglected cock slapped against his stomach. Masuo's pace increased, and he reached down and grasped Hayato's hard length. Hayato let out a choked groan.

"You're going to come for me," Masuo hissed.

Hayato moaned something incomprehensible, but with a final shallow thrust of Masuo's hips, he was pushed over the edge. He came, hot and wet, and the clench of Hayato's muscles milked Masuo to his own finish.

Masuo took a few deep breaths and unlocked the handcuffs, rubbing at Hayato's hands to get the blood flowing again. Then Masuo grabbed a stack of napkins leftover from his take-out dinner and cleaned up Hayato while he took care of the mess on the sofa.

A sigh of contentment left Masuo, and Hayato pulled Masuo onto the couch. He couldn't have asked for anything else in life besides a good job and someone he loved.

Masuo's hand trailed over the scar running down Hayato's stomach.

"How did you get this?" Masuo asked.

"You really want to know?" It sounded like a dare.

"I want to know everything about you."

Hayato snorted. "Don't say I didn't warn you. You heard about the Yamashita ward massacre?"

"A little bit."

"The Korean mafia rammed into the safe-house garage. They spilled out like a smashed bottle of wine. My brother and I were on the second story, so we had a few extra moments to prepare and put together a quick plan."

Masuo hugged Hayato a little closer, glad he'd opened himself up to share the painful memory.

Hayato wet his lips. "I ended up getting into a knife fight with one of them. I was lucky to survive with only this cut. Subaru grabbed some newspaper and pressed it so hard the ink came off on my skin anyplace not covered in blood. I think he was scared my organs would fall out. He took me to a yakuza-friendly doctor. Subaru didn't have a scratch. So like him."

"I'm glad you made it out all right."

"My brother and I were the only survivors. They gave

us a huge bonus and set us up with easy jobs as payment. An ugly scar might not be a bad trade-off."

Masuo traced the line of the scar. "I don't think it's ugly. It makes you look tough."

Hayato laughed. "Tough is the last thing I look."

"It's like you said at the apartment viewing. You use the fact you don't look tough to your advantage when people underestimate you."

"Yeah, then I kick their asses."

Masuo rested his head on Hayato's shoulder. A nagging feeling clawed at him. He was twenty and finally cultivating the life he'd always wanted, but one thing kept nipping at him like a gnat in a room.

"Have you ever thought about getting married and having kids?" Masuo asked, using all the courage within him.

"Have I ever told you how massive your cock is?"

"Why do you always switch to sex every time I want to talk about something serious?"

Hayato sighed. "I'm gay, Masuo."

"I know."

"So I don't think a bunch of crusty old politicians that think I'm the cause of the low birth rate will suddenly think it's a good idea to allow me to marry."

"Come on. The whole world is changing. They only reason it's a big deal here is because of the Meiji Restoration."

Hayato put his fingers to Masuo's lips. "You're bi, so you can think about a family and marriage. The closest I've come is thinking about being the cool uncle that buys my brother's offspring drinks."

"But if the law did change, would you want to?"

"I'm not going to lie to you."

Masuo's heart broke. "So that's a no."

Hayato sighed. "It's an I don't know. Ask me when the law changes. It's not like I grew up with a shiny example of marriage."

It wasn't a no, and Hayato was right. It wasn't until Murata had become godfather that Masuo had thought it was possible to be himself. But why couldn't his desire for marriage and kids be a goal with a man or a woman? His parents had met when they were his age. They'd gotten engaged a year later, then married the year after that. Masuo wanted to make sure whoever he was in a relationship with wanted the same thing.

"So we're not going to go for three rounds." Hayato looked down at Masuo's soft cock.

He laughed. "Maybe once I get Mondays off again."

"In a few months, then."

"Months? I was hoping to get days off after my huge profits start rolling in following the grand reopening."

"You wish."

"I'm at least on the right track," Masuo said. "You've been collecting money every day since I made that deal with the nightclub."

"Sure, maybe you're turning this place into a popular spot, but you only get that day off if I say so."

"Hmm, then I better make sure to treat you right."

"If we have more days like today, then you'll have no issues getting Mondays off." Hayato's fingers trailed against Masuo's cheek. "First the phone sex, and now the cop yakuza role-play. It's like you know all my kinks."

"Well, you did make a list for me." Masuo laughed, but Hayato's face remained blank. The little jab of playful tease to get Masuo over his heartache melted. "You don't remember the list, do you?"

"I was drinking." Hayato shrugged, and the last touch of euphoria shattered.

"Should I assume you don't remember anything when you drink?"

"Usually I'm fine, but January is a hard month. I let myself drink a little too much. It happens."

Masuo's muscles tensed, and staying so close to Hayato grew to feel too much like a lie. Masuo stood and ripped the list from the notebook on the desk. He crumpled it up and tossed it at Hayato.

"I thought we were going down the list the whole time," Masuo said.

"I'm sorry." Hayato sounded sincere, but it didn't soothe the burn in Masuo's heart. "I can bring you naked breakfast in bed tomorrow morning."

"I don't want it like that." Masuo shook his head. "You don't get it. I want someone who remembers our evenings together. Someone who will be there for me and is willing to sacrifice. Maybe we aren't meant—"

"I love you."

Masuo's mouth dropped open, but he was too shocked to speak.

"I love you," Hayato repeated. "Please, don't..."

His eyes turned glassy and wet, like he'd finally opened himself up to something raw and true for the first time, and it pained him.

The confession sent Masuo's world asunder like a cheap umbrella caught in a typhoon. He'd been ready to call the whole thing off, but now... When he looked into Hayato's eyes, he knew his confessed words were true, but when Masuo thought of Hayato and their relationship, the future felt too foggy to see. It wasn't love, at least not yet, but he did feel something.

Masuo pressed his lips together and took Hayato's hand in his. "I felt our bond the first night when you held my hand. I'm not sure how I feel, but I'm curious to see where it leads."

During the whole walk to Subaru's, Hayato couldn't get Masuo out of his head. Yesterday, the confession of love had leaped from Hayato's throat and had taken a swan dive to the parlor's concrete floor. Sure, the words helped solve the problem in the short term, but why had he said them? Did he love Masuo? When had that happened? They had only known each other for two weeks. Could you love someone after two weeks? They were just having fun, right? But then why had Hayato's insides been crushed when Masuo hadn't said "I love you" back? Even thinking about it sent Hayato's heart aching like it had been steamrolled into oblivion.

January made everything so damn complicated.

Hayato knocked on Subaru's door, but Fumiko answered.

She pulled Hayato into an embrace like they hadn't seen each other in years when it had been a week. The only new things in the apartment were a few pictures of the couple and a bar cart stocked with alcohol in the far corner.

"You like the apartment so far?" Hayato asked.

"It's perfect." A honeymoon glow beamed from Fumiko's smile.

Subaru could've decorated the place with his smelly socks, and she would've said the same thing.

"You want a drink?" Fumiko asked.

"Your cocktails are always delicious."

Hayato scooted into the kitchen and saw Subaru loading the last of some pork buns inside a bamboo steamer. Hayato handed him the lid so he could say he helped out.

"Is she a better roommate than me?" he asked.

"Having Fumiko around does come with more perks." Subaru laughed and gave his brother a warm hug.

They chatted about work while the buns steamed. Fumiko's choice of cocktail was bright orange with a zesty, fresh aftertaste. She and Subaru worked together to get the table set. Hayato could only smile. Maybe one day he and Masuo would be at a point where they knew what the other was thinking. Hayato bit the inside of his cheek. There he was, thinking about Masuo again. He'd been the perfect boyfriend even when Hayato had fucked up and couldn't remember something important to him. Hayato would have to try harder if he wanted something as solid as what Fumiko and Subaru had.

Subaru brought the steamer to the table and gave Fumiko the first bun.

"The new apartment going good?" Subaru asked.

"I love it. There's always activity going on in the lounge. It's perfect."

"So next week we'll eat at your place?"

"Maybe in a few weeks. I'm still getting used to it. When's the next competition?" Hayato hoped getting them to talk about dancing would get their minds off him.

"We have a little hop happening later tonight, but the real start of the season is next week," Fumiko said. "With all the moving, we decided to go freestyle so we wouldn't need to practice anything."

Hayato nodded. "Sometimes it's good to take a break."

She looked at Subaru and gave a half smile. They were planning something. Had Subaru dropped by his apartment unannounced and seen how empty it was? Hayato could say all the furniture he liked was on back order. He couldn't let Subaru worry. Not when he had such a good thing with Fumiko.

"So the twenty-second is coming up," Subaru said, his tone rehearsed. "I know we usually visit Mother's grave together, but..."

Fumiko picked it up from there. "I was hoping I could visit her grave with you. Would that be okay?"

Steam rose out of Hayato's half-eaten bun. He closed his eyes. It was only six days away. The weight bore down on his shoulders and wrapped around his neck. The day was so close. And Fumiko wanted to join in like it was some fun family tradition?

"Why would you want to go to something so depressing?" Hayato asked.

"I don't think it's depressing. I help my parents clean our family grave every year. Subaru joined us last year, and it was nice." She interlaced her fingers with Subaru's.

"I took off the day, so whatever time works for you," Subaru added.

Of course she would want to come with Subaru. They were becoming a family, and visiting graves would become a tradition just like the weekly dinners.

Subaru was getting a handle on his life. Hayato should too. He didn't want to intrude. He should be building his own independence and allowing his brother the chance at happiness.

"This year, I want to try going by myself." Hayato hoped the words came out stronger than he felt.

"We've gone together every year." Subaru's eyes narrowed. "Is it because Fumiko wants to come? She doesn't have to. That's why she's asking if it's okay with you first."

"I know your mother was special to you both. That's why I wanted to go," Fumiko added. "But I can stay behind."

Hayato didn't know if she knew how bad his monophobia was or if Subaru had even mentioned it. Or maybe they both weren't even thinking about it. The one time Subaru believed one of Hayato's lies, and it was the biggest one.

"I don't care that she's coming." The words came out harsher than he intended. "Sorry, what I mean is, I need to learn to do things by myself."

Subaru opened his mouth, then closed it, his face turning expressionless. He couldn't argue with Hayato finally trying to live like a normal person who wasn't scared he'd die without someone else there.

"If you want to go by yourself, that's fine, but I'm

going to ask you again the day before in case you change your mind."

"This is something I've been thinking over for a while," Hayato lied, but it would keep Subaru from worrying.

If Hayato could make it through the worst day of the year without needing his brother's companionship, then maybe Hayato could finally start a real life on his own. Furniture shopping wouldn't feel so impossible. Maybe all the future planning Masuo had talked about would become his dream too.

Hayato finished the last of his pork buns. "I gotta go to work."

"Can I walk with you to the station?" Subaru asked.

"Sure." If Hayato said no, he'd never hear the end of it.

They grabbed their coats and headed out. Subaru didn't speak, probably because he always waited for the awkward silence to grow so uncomfortable Hayato would break first.

"How did you know Fumiko was the right person?" The question flew out of Hayato's mouth without a thought. He needed to get a handle on that or the next thing he knew, he'd be the one asking for Masuo's hand.

"I knew she was the right person when I couldn't stop thinking about her," Subaru said.

"Do you love her?"

"Of course."

"When did you tell her?"

Subaru's breath fogged around him as he let out a deep sigh. "About a year ago."

"Did you tell her as soon as you knew?"

Subaru grinned. "You're sure asking a lot of love questions. You've been with a lot of guys. Haven't you loved some of them? Or is something different about Masuo?"

Hayato swore one day he'd learn Subaru's super secret I-know-everything-about-you powers. Maybe it came from his extra three minutes of life.

"Well?" Subaru pressed.

"I kind of blurted out that I loved him."

"And what did he say?"

"He didn't say it back, if that's what you're asking."

"That must've hurt," Subaru said. "But you'd want him to be honest about it, right?"

"With my exes, they said it first, and I said it back. At the time, I thought I meant it, but now..." Hayato rubbed his chest. "I'm not sure if that was true. Did I love them, or did I love their company, or did I just love fucking them? I mean, I told Jiro I loved him, but we ended up being horrible for each other."

"Is that why you're working so hard to get over your monophobia? So you can make sure what you feel for Masuo is real?"

A tingling tickled at the back of Hayato's throat. Hayato wasn't sure. All his feelings had become a jumbled ball of confusion. January sucked, and the closer it got to the anniversary of his mother's death, the more confusing everything got.

"If it helps any, I knew I loved Fumiko after a month," Subaru said. "I didn't tell her, but I would show her. Sometimes I think the only reason I said it was because there were rumors about the Korean mob wanting to take

Kyoto. I wanted her to know in case something happened."

"But like..." Hayato pressed his lips together and wished his heart would stop aching. "You and Fumiko are perfect for each other. How did you know it would work?"

"It's a relationship. It takes two people trying to make it work. It's more than knowing that I love her. She challenges and pushes me to become a better person. She wants me to become the best version of myself I can be, and I want her to be the best Fumiko she can be." Subaru shook his head and laughed. "This might be all the swing competition stuff talking."

"It makes sense."

Hayato could push Masuo to be a better parlor manager, and so far Masuo had pushed Hayato to care more about their relationship and not only focus on how they were in bed.

"I know you always say whatever's on your mind, so if you told Masuo you love him, then I think that's truly how you feel."

Hayato crossed his arms. "Now you're working on getting the best brother of the year award."

"Maybe Masuo wouldn't mind visiting Mom's grave. Then all four of us can go together."

"On the worst double date ever? You totally lost your position for that award."

Subaru chuckled. "I'm sure I'll earn it back."

"I need..." Hayato bit his lip. "It's time I learn to be by myself."

"You already have your own place. You've been there a whole week. You're already doing it." Subaru gave Hayato a big hug. "I'm proud of you. I know Mom would be too. Don't be so hard on yourself."

If only he knew how badly Hayato had screwed up living alone.

HAYATO RUBBED his lower back and leaned against the side of the van. Masuo had taken the keys with him as he signed the car rental paperwork. If only he'd remembered to unlock the van before, the frigid January night might be a little more bearable.

Masuo left the rental center, jingling the keys in his hand.

"You got the one with heated seats?" Hayato half joked. He doubted any van had heated seats, but it would've been nice.

"You'll be warm in no time."

Masuo blasted the heat, which only circulated the freezing air.

"This isn't working," Hayato said. "Are you sure it's not broken?"

"Give it a few minutes."

"I know a way you can warm me up real fast." Hayato glanced toward the back filled with blankets to cushion the pachinko machines.

"Tall Ken is expecting us."

"He'll be there all night. We've got time."

Masuo laughed like Hayato had told a joke.

By the time they turned onto the highway, heat blew from the vents. Hayato took his hands out of his pockets and pressed them against his thighs.

With only four days before the parlor's grand reopening, Hayato should've been happy Masuo had allowed him to tag along and distract him with dirty jokes.

"I should have enough to get five new machines," Masuo said. "If I stick them by the front, I think I'll attract more people."

"Sounds like a plan."

Masuo talked more about ads and how the deal he'd struck with the club's manager was gaining momentum. Hayato tried to pay attention. Getting the parlor up to snuff was what Masuo was interested in. If it was important to him, it was important to Hayato, but then Masuo started talking about increases in return rates and gross profits to the third decimal point.

"What kind of music do you like?" Hayato asked.

"Rock."

"Good, me too." Hayato clicked on the radio and flipped through the stations.

"Okay, okay. I get it. I'll stop talking about the parlor."

Hayato switched off the radio. "Good because I thought the stock market station had been left on."

Masuo hid a laugh behind a playful smile.

"Did you get everything with your apartment situated?" Masuo asked.

"It's pretty much the same."

"You haven't bought any furniture?"

"I bought a futon, sure, but now I think I want a Western bed. Then I need to get a bed frame, and do the sheets need to match the curtains then? It's so much I don't know what to get."

The apartment had turned into nothing more than an

expensive closet. Hayato would go to work, then finish the day by circling back to hang out as Masuo painted or tweaked the machines. If Hayato was lucky, Masuo would agree to a movie, but the past few days, it had been too close to the reopening for him to stay out late. So Hayato would head home, change, and go to the bar. Once that closed, he'd head to the manga café, where he'd accidentally fall asleep, since he'd been banned from the apartment's lounge.

"You seem like someone who knows their style," Masuo said.

"Clothes, sure, but furniture? It's like being abandoned on a different planet." Hayato adjusted one of Masuo's vents to face him. Masuo never complained about the cold, so he wouldn't mind.

"Maybe you need someone to give you a second opinion. I can go with you. My apartment furniture might be crappy, but I have more than you, it seems."

"I can't ask you to gallivant around furniture stores while I find my style. You have more important things to do with the parlor."

"All the more reason to make sure my ideas are good. Then I can make enough profit for that day off, and you can ask me to go without feeling guilty."

"Fine, fine. All your ideas for the opening sound phenomenal. I didn't even need to show you the ropes, since you already knew what had to be done. Endo threw you in the deep end, and you learned to swim. You're not an incompetent person who's only good at breaking figurines." Hayato laughed.

"Hey!" Masuo poked Hayato while trying to keep his eyes on the road.

Had they not been driving, Hayato could've seen the poking turning into tickling and some long kisses. But they were driving, so it only turned into a few giggles and a happy sigh from Masuo.

"You said January was a hard month for you." Masuo reached over, took Hayato's hand, and gave it a tight squeeze. "I'm here for you."

Hayato let out a wry smile. First Subaru wanted to bring it up, now Masuo.

"If you ever need someone to talk—"

"It was the worst day of my life. Talking about it is the last thing I want to do." Hayato's tone was biting, but Masuo didn't withdraw his hand, and Hayato didn't let go.

All Hayato's other exes had either not lasted long enough or were too self-absorbed to notice Hayato's uptick in January drinking. Really, that alone should've earned Masuo the number one boyfriend ranking.

Hayato clutched onto Masuo's hand, his thumb rubbing up and down the side of his palm. Masuo was impossible. How could someone be so good, especially when Hayato knew he'd been kind of a jerk?

"My parents and I used to go camping all the time when I was little," Masuo said, changing topics. "We'd even bring our cats."

"What?" Hayato shook his head. "A dog I get, but cats? They don't want to be there."

"They liked being outside. I would take them on hikes on a leash and everything."

"I don't believe it."

"My mom has pictures. Photo albums, even, if you want to see."

"Little Masuo must've been adorable."

"I had the most awkward bowl cut."

Hayato laughed. "My mom made us rock the bowl cut too."

"I kept mine until I went to high school."

"We all have flaws. I used to sing American pop music in the school halls, horribly off-key."

Hayato sang a few bars of a song, but with the decade between them, Masuo would only recognize it from the dance remix.

"Did your parents ever take you camping?" Masuo asked.

"Are you trying to get my gay ass to go camping?"

"It might be nice when it gets warm."

"I haven't been camping in my life. We'd skip the small vacations for trips to America."

"Oh, fancy. I haven't ever been outside Japan."

"My mom taught English, and the company my dad worked for had strong ties in America," Hayato said. "Usually we'd tag along on his business trips, then stay longer for a family vacation."

"That must've been fun."

"Kind of." Hayato squeezed Masuo's hand. "They made us speak English the whole time. Sometimes I wouldn't be able to understand a menu and would get stuck with awful things like chicken fried chicken. I still don't even know what I ended up eating."

"So your vacation was one big English class assignment?"

"Basically. It's what happens when your mom's a teacher."

They chatted more, the conversation flowing easily and not in any way related to work.

Masuo turned off onto a side street and pulled up to a warehouse in the middle of nowhere. Masuo would probably never understand how much Hayato enjoyed his company, and not just as a distraction from the month. They did have good chemistry.

"This should be it," Masuo said.

"Looks about right."

Masuo parked, and all the warmth in the van left the second he opened the door. He could've at least given Hayato some goodbye time with the heat.

They got out and wandered around to the back of the warehouse. Masuo tottered off ahead, not caring that Hayato's hands were freezing. He would've welcomed a warm hand to hold. Hayato chalked it up to Masuo's sheer enthusiasm for parlor improvements.

"Hello?" Masuo called. "I'm here to see Tall Ken about some pachinko machines."

Ken came out, eyes narrowed, like he was ready for a fight. He looked like he hadn't shaved in a week, his facial hair grown out in awkward patches.

"Who are you?" Ken grunted.

"I'm Masuo from Kyoto, and this is Hayato. I have been talking with Tall Ken for the past week."

"Hey, Ken." Hayato waved.

Ken crossed his arms. "You're late."

"There was some traffic."

Ken rolled his eyes. "Knowing Hayato, he got bored and demanded a blow job."

Hayato wrapped his arms around Masuo. "I don't think about sex all the time."

Ken looked at Masuo. "Don't believe anything he says. Last time we went out to a club together, I shit glitter for a week."

Masuo raised a brow.

"Ken used to be the best go-go dancer at a bar I went to a few years back," Hayato said. "He used to get on the pole and do some awesome moves. One time, he even stuck—"

"No need to go down memory lane," Ken said. "Come on. The machines are this way."

They followed Ken, and Masuo asked a million questions about the machines. He even made Ken plug each one in so Masuo could test them. They were diamonds compared to the shit Masuo had been given. The lights glittered in a rainbow of colors, and the large LCD screens played videos with enough bouncing-boobed characters to have any straight man sitting there for hours.

Ken sauntered over to where Hayato waited.

"The guy's picky." Ken jutted his stubbly chin at Masuo.

"He's into his job."

"You still dating that loser Jiro?"

"I'm with Masuo now."

Ken whistled. "Didn't see that coming."

"What?"

"He must have a huge dick to keep your attention."

"We haven't talked in two years, and this is what you want to discuss?" Hayato crossed his arms.

"I know you, and I can't see it lasting more than a month."

"Fuck you. You don't know anything about Masuo."

"He's playing every machine. I think I even saw him write down the serial numbers."

"I like that he's into his job."

"Again, I give it a month before you get bored and are back at the club looking for company. The only reason you were with Jiro for so long was because of his penthouse, and this guy doesn't strike me as someone into luxury."

Ken had known Hayato for a while, and sure, they'd had a falling out a while back, but hearing the words struck Hayato's core. He'd gone to the clubs for company so he wouldn't have to face being alone. He swallowed. He wasn't that person anymore. He had his own place. He was getting over his fear.

"I'll take five," Masuo said, finally finished with his test run.

He and Ken haggled while Hayato stewed. He and Masuo would last longer than a month. Masuo was already talking about what they would do during the spring, not to mention his whole married-with-kids fantasy.

Though with the shitty things Ken had been saying, Masuo was probably having second thoughts about their relationship. Masuo wanted someone who would sacrifice. Hayato could do that.

"How much for the lot of them?" Hayato asked.

Ken laughed.

"I'm serious. We'll take as many as you can fit in the van."

Masuo pulled Hayato to the side and kept his voice low. "What are you doing?"

"You worked hard to get the parlor the way it is now. Why can't I help you make it what you wanted?"

"You don't have to."

"But I want to, and this way you'll get that Monday off sooner." Hayato winked.

A crease formed in the center of Masuo's forehead. Why wouldn't he let him help?

"Look, I know you used your own income to help buy the machines. What's the difference between you doing it and me doing it?" Hayato asked.

"I need to show Endo I'm not some incompetent bastard who breaks things."

"Is that why you're refusing help?" Hayato held on to Masuo's hand. "You've already impressed me. Endo only looks at your numbers each day, not at all the things you've already done to improve the parlor. She'll be impressed by the profit you make. The newer the machines, the more profit. Only then will she see the good businessman I know you already are."

Masuo shook his head. "But it's so expensive."

"How about you buy five and I'll buy five?"

Masuo looked toward the machines. He would have to be stupid not to take the deal, but maybe offering to help wounded his pride too much.

"Only if you make it a formal loan," he said, like it was the last thing he wanted. "We'll draw up paperwork and use our seals and everything."

"But they're a gift. I want to give them to you so you can be the best businessman you can."

Masuo shook his head. "Then gift me a fancy new ledger or more notebooks so I can write to-do lists. I want to earn my day off, not have it bought for me."

He was the most stubborn man Hayato had ever met. "Fine. It's a loan. Do you want the standard ten percent interest every ten days?"

"Maybe that part can be a boyfriend discount."

Hayato gave Masuo a quick peck on the lips. "That's what I thought, love cookie."

"I said no food, remember?" Masuo laughed. "Maybe we can do something easy and think of a cute way to say each other's names."

"We can do better than that. We've got the whole ride back to come up with something better."

18

If January was the worst month of the year, then the twenty-second was the worst day. Hayato could hardly believe he'd made it to seven in the morning without crawling to his brother for support. If Subaru was fine spending the day by himself, Hayato could be too. Only seventeen hours left to prove he could make it by himself, but the doubt he would make it had already sunk deep into his bones. Especially since Masuo had picked today out of all 365 available days for his grand reopening of the parlor. He'd already made it clear he'd be too exhausted from the day to be there when Hayato needed companionship the most.

Hayato rolled up a flyer and wedged it into his neighbor's door handle. The bright-orange paper would be impossible to ignore. Inside, it announced the first meeting of the newly formed movie club. If he invited everyone in the building, management would never find out it was him. And if he attended, he'd simply be following the crowd. They couldn't get mad at him for joining in.

He kept his thoughts on his actions because he simply couldn't trust himself otherwise.

Grab a movie club flyer from the stack.

Roll it up.

Wedge it in the door handle.

Move on to the next door.

Grab a paper…

With the last flyer stuck into the handle on the last door, Hayato joined the crowds of people heading to the train station. Most were dressed in business attire, as was Hayato, having used his apartment as a closet again.

The early morning rush hour proved another way to keep his deeper thoughts at bay. He kept to surface-level details, cataloging the styles of the suits and coats the other men wore.

Hayato pushed himself onto the train, avoiding the stop at a florist until it became unavoidable. People crowded around him and stuffed the train like neatly packed sushi.

He pulled out his phone and poked around, mirroring the others around him.

Nothing new.

Nothing to distract him.

At least Masuo would have a good day. He'd planned everything for the parlor's grand reopening in such sickeningly specific detail it could only be successful.

Before, Hayato had thought Masuo was some cocky twenty-year-old who couldn't even begin to realize how woefully ignorant he was about working a successful pachinko parlor. Yet his youthful drive had pushed him to heights Hayato had never imagined. His first memory was thinking about how clingy Masuo was, but every day since they'd become official, Hayato had been clinging to Masuo for company.

The train slowed to a stop, and the exchange of people coming and going left Hayato with new faces to distract him, but it only lasted for a few minutes.

Hayato closed his eyes. The day would end. Somehow.

"Hey," Masuo said.

Hayato opened his eyes, almost doubting that the voice he heard was indeed Masuo's, but there he stood. He stood so close their bodies brushed up against each other. The train was so packed everyone touched. He wore the same suit he'd worn on his first day. It hugged every curve of his body and made it easy for Hayato to mentally undress him.

"What are you doing here?" Hayato kept his voice low, not wanting to disturb the people around him.

"Going to the parlor."

"But it doesn't open for another three hours."

"I couldn't sleep." Masuo shrugged. "Figured I might as well get things set up."

"You need to take care of yourself or else you'll burn out."

Masuo laughed. "Well, it made me run into you. So that's good."

"Yeah, and now we can both be squished."

"There are some advantages to that too."

Masuo brushed against Hayato's crotch. It felt like a mistake at first, but then his hand stayed, deliberately rubbing against the fabric of the long coat in slow, rough strokes. The rush of possibly being seen sent a tingling wave of electricity through Hayato. He suppressed a moan and unbuttoned his long coat, allowing Masuo's hand closer and giving them a bit more camouflage for the hand job.

A part of Hayato still couldn't believe Masuo was ready to continue down the list after Hayato had forgotten the initial exchange. Hopefully it was a sign of forgiveness. Though, perhaps Masuo was just excited to push his sexual boundaries a little more.

"How adventurous do you think you can be?" Hayato dared.

A glint flashed in Masuo's sandy-brown eyes, and a little smirk crossed his face. The next instant, Hayato's zipper was down, the separation of each tooth ringing clearer than if it had come from the loudspeaker.

The distraction was more perfect than anything Hayato could've come up with. He closed his eyes, slid his hands into his coat pockets, and held out the ends to give them a little more cover. Not everyone would enjoy the show. Masuo took the invitation to explore further. After a few more rubs of his palm, his fingers slipped inside. He pushed back the fabric of Hayato's underwear to expose his hardening cock.

Masuo's cold fingers sent a chill up Hayato's spine. Masuo's long, teasing strokes pushed all the horrible thoughts aside. Through the hell of January, with all its ups and downs, Masuo had been there. Hayato doubted he would've been able to make it this far without him.

The overhead voice called out the next station, and the train slowed.

"You got me excited," Hayato whispered in Masuo's ear. "Do you want more?"

Masuo nodded.

"Me too."

Hayato buttoned up his coat so it hid his crotch. A little moan escaped the back of his throat as the soft woolen fabric brushed against his sensitive length. Then, once the train stopped, Hayato grabbed Masuo's hand and led him to the restrooms. Masuo pushed open the door to the larger stall and locked it behind them.

Everything became a blur of movement and heat even though Hayato wanted it slow, but dirty public-restroom sex wasn't meant to be romantic.

Masuo unbuckled his pants and pulled them down. He braced himself against the door, pushing his hips out. The tails of his white collared shirt didn't quite cover his toned ass. A flush of goose bumps formed on Masuo's skin. He looked back at Hayato with a pleading look, begging to be touched.

Hayato kissed the back of Masuo's neck, trailing up before he nipped at his ear.

"I want you," Masuo whispered with a little grunt.

"You'll want me more if we take our time."

Hayato turned Masuo so he could deepen the kiss. His tongue traced Hayato's lips until they opened, but Masuo took it slow and sweet. Hayato's heart welcomed the tender affection. He owed the man so much for putting up with him in the chaos of January, for somehow being there in the darkest hours of the day. While Masuo still hadn't returned Hayato's words of love, Hayato felt the strength of their bond in the kiss.

Masuo moaned and grasped at Hayato's length before

rubbing and cupping his balls and rolling them across his palm. A small whimper escaped as he ground against Hayato.

"I want you in me." Masuo's husky voice curled Hayato's toes. "I want you to fuck me so hard I can't sit down without thinking of you."

Hayato licked his lips, a shiver of anticipation rippling through him. "I don't have any condoms."

"I don't care."

"You sure?"

"If you make me wait any longer, I'm going to explode."

Hayato cracked a smile, eager to please. Masuo reached into his pocket and pushed a tube of lube into Hayato's hand.

"You always carry lube?" Hayato teased.

"We used up what I had at the parlor when we played cop and yakuza."

Masuo put his hands against the door and looked back at Hayato. "Hurry."

Hayato had never heard a single word said with such sheer eroticism, but hurrying was the last thing Hayato was planning to do. If he could, he'd make their bathroom tryst last all day, all month.

Hayato snapped the top, and the distinct scent of peppermint permeated the air. He narrowed his eyes at the bottle that had a few swirled red candies pictured on the front.

"You bought flavored lube?" Hayato chuckled.

Masuo wiggled his butt. "It's supposed to tingle."

Hayato put a generous amount on his fingers. The thick liquid wasn't bad at all once the strong scent mellowed out. Hayato pressed a finger against Masuo's hole.

"Does it tingle?" Hayato asked.

"A little. I think I'll feel it more if you actually stick it in me."

"Hmm."

Hayato teased a little more before finally slipping a finger inside. It went in easily, and Masuo let out a little choked noise. His muscles twitched, and Hayato slid out his finger before pushing in a little farther.

"I want to hear you," Hayato said.

"Someone might..."

"Isn't that half the fun?"

Hayato kneeled, pulling Masuo's cheeks apart before diving his tongue inside. Masuo let out a rolling moan so loud it echoed in the small space. Each grateful cry from Masuo's lips sent a wave of pleasure through Hayato as well. He wanted to lavish ecstasy on Masuo so he'd understand how desperately Hayato needed him. How thankful he was Masuo was a part of his life. At first, Hayato might've shouted out his words of love so they wouldn't break up, but they were true. Their love, unbreakable—more so than ever—and the sheer, pure pleasure of each shallow groan escaping Masuo's mouth proved their bond.

"I want you in me," Masuo panted out between grunts.

"I am in you."

"Bastard," Masuo said under his breath, making Hayato grin.

He stood and poured another generous amount of

lube on his cock. He pressed the tip to Masuo's entrance but didn't slide in.

"Why don't you tell me exactly what you want," Hayato said.

Masuo's legs trembled, his eyes shining with lust. "Impale me with your cock."

The toilet in the stall beside them flushed, and Masuo's cheeks reddened, but in that second, Hayato entered him fully, and Masuo was back to moaning like they were the only people in the world. His back arched, meeting each of Hayato's thrusts. He was balls deep in Masuo.

Their lovemaking was hard and raw and everything Masuo wanted. Hayato didn't need to remember the day. He could lose himself in Masuo, and he did everything to push them both over the edge. Masuo clenched his muscles around Hayato, and the tingle from the peppermint lube did not go unnoticed. It teased Hayato's cock as shamelessly as Masuo's moans. Hayato could feel himself drawing close, his thrusts becoming frantic and losing the slow, punishingly deliberate rhythm against Masuo's most tantalizing spot.

"Claim me," Masuo cried.

The words alone drove Hayato over the edge, and Masuo followed quickly after. Hayato gasped for breath and held on to the stall wall for support.

"That was so incredibly sexy." Masuo grabbed some toilet paper.

Hayato nodded, but as he sank to the floor, everything hit him at once. Masuo would be on the next train going to the parlor, starting the day that would probably be one of his happiest, and then what would Hayato do? Hayato would continue reliving one of his worst days. He swallowed hard, almost regretting that Masuo had found him.

"Hey, you okay?" Masuo squatted to meet Hayato's gaze.

Masuo's sandy eyes filled with worry. Hayato looked away, tugging on his fuzzy coat sleeve. He wanted to say he was fine, but the lie wouldn't leave his mouth.

"My treasure..."

Hearing their decided pet name for each other hurt worse. Hayato closed his eyes tight, hoping to stop the pain inside his heart from leaking out.

"What's wrong?" Masuo squeezed Hayato's knee.

"It's..." How could he even begin to explain everything? "Will you come with me somewhere?"

"Sure. We can go tomorrow."

Hayato's lip trembled, and Masuo met his gaze. Masuo wrapped his arms around him, and inside that secure hug, Hayato broke. He let out an agonized cry fueled by the pain of twenty years.

"It's okay." Masuo squeezed Hayato's hand. "Tell me what's bothering you?"

"I can't visit my mother's grave alone."

19

Hayato's words reached out like an icy hand and throttled Masuo's thoughts. It left them atrophying in the space between his brain and his mouth. He could only stand there dumbfounded while Hayato struggled to stifle his cries echoing around the small restroom. Tears stained his cheeks. Masuo embraced him, hoping it would somehow convey all the words of comfort he couldn't piece together.

He had been so wrong. Hayato didn't drink to forget their evenings but to forget his mother's death. A wound that was raw and festering no matter how many years had passed.

"I can't do it alone. I thought I could, but I can't. I just can't." Hayato buried his head in Masuo's arms.

Masuo squeezed Hayato tighter, hoping it helped somehow. Masuo's heart ached. He didn't want Hayato to hurt.

Then it hit Masuo like a lightning strike. He felt helpless and at a loss for how to help because he wanted

Hayato. He wanted to be Hayato's North Star. His light in the cruel darkness. His one and only.

Today.

Tomorrow.

Forever.

"I love you," Masuo said. The words felt freeing, like stepping off a cliff knowing Hayato would be there to catch him.

But Hayato kept crying. Had he not heard Masuo's words? Wouldn't knowing Masuo loved him help? Masuo swallowed and rubbed Hayato's back.

"I love you," Masuo repeated louder. "You don't have to go alone because I'll go with you."

Hayato pulled back, his eyes swollen and red. "You have the opening. You won't make it back in time. Her grave is outside the city."

"You're more important to me than the opening." No words felt truer as Masuo said them.

"But you've been planning it for weeks. You don't have to do this."

"That's what you do for people you love. You make sacrifices when they need you."

Hayato didn't move. He didn't speak, but Masuo would stay by his side as long as it took. They loved each other and could work through their problems together.

"I'll try to get you back in time." Hayato's voice sounded meek.

"You set the pace for this. Don't worry about the time."

Masuo stood and held out his hand to Hayato. He let out a deep sigh that carried more weight than Masuo could understand, but Hayato took his hand.

"Let's do this," he said.

Hayato cleaned himself up, and they got back on the train.

The crowds thinned more the longer they stayed. Eventually two seats opened up, and they went from standing next to each other to sitting side by side.

"Sorry it's taking forever. Mom grew up outside the city. Dad thought she'd want—" Hayato bit his lip.

They were in public, so embracing would be out of the question. Instead, Masuo stretched out his legs and pressed his polished black shoe next to Hayato's. He smiled, though it was marred with worry.

Masuo's great-grandmother had died when he was a kid. They hadn't been close, but he'd always enjoyed hearing the happy memories his mom would share. Maybe it would help Hayato to focus on the good.

"You said your mom taught English?" Masuo asked.

"At the high school."

"English was my worst subject."

"I was pretty good at it. When I was young, I wanted to be a teacher like her. Not so much after she..." Hayato sighed. "I would hear English and think of her."

"That would be difficult." Masuo wanted Hayato to think of happy memories, not hard ones. Maybe he'd been going about it the wrong way. "I'd like to know more about her."

"She was always dressed nicely."

"She's where you got your fashion sense?"

A faint smile crossed Hayato's face. "She was way more into brands than I am. She'd buy fashion magazines, then buy knockoffs once they hit the department stores. I buy whatever I think looks nice. I don't think I ever saw her without lipstick. She would always kiss my dad on the cheek before he left for work, and she'd leave a lipstick mark on him. When we were little, Subaru and I would giggle about it, and my dad would pretend he didn't know why."

Masuo laughed. "She must've been a great mother."

"She was. Well, when she wasn't sick."

The announcement for the next station sounded, and Hayato stood. "This is our stop."

They got off the train at one of the towns outside Kyoto. They picked up some flowers and incense along the way to the cemetery.

The morning sun warmed Masuo's face. The chirping birds flew around the leafless trees. It might've been any sunny winter's day, but somehow, so far away from the city and his parlor, it felt surreal.

Masuo glanced around, checking the street was abandoned before taking hold of Hayato's hand. Their fingers laced together, and Hayato held on tight. Maybe Masuo shouldn't have needed to look around before showing his affection. When he'd freaked out on the stairs, Hayato hadn't cared what the manager thought about their clasped hands.

"Subaru and I usually come together," Hayato said. "This year I tried to convince myself I could do it alone. I was stupid to think I could."

"You're not stupid. Sometimes people need help."

Hayato's fingers curled, crinkling the plastic wrap around the flowers he held in his other hand. "I need to learn how to do things on my own at some point."

Masuo raised a brow, but Hayato didn't say anything more for the next few blocks.

The black pillar graves rose on the hill ahead. Hayato didn't let go of Masuo's hand until they reached the cemetery entrance.

Hayato grabbed one of the offered wooden buckets and filled it with water, while Masuo washed his hands and mouth.

"It's this way," Hayato said.

They plodded along down the rows of pillars until Hayato came to a stop. The grave had a few overgrown weeds among the stones. Together they cleaned the grave, pouring water over the black pillar stone, then scrubbing it clean.

Hayato lit the incense and put the flowers in one of the vases flanking the center stone. Hayato clapped, saying a quick prayer before Masuo repeated the motions.

Hayato took in a deep breath and stared at the grave. "I'm actually the age she was. In May, I'll be older. How is that supposed to work? I can't be older than my mother."

Masuo pressed his lips together, not sure how to respond. He took a step closer to Hayato so Hayato would know he was there, but Hayato kept staring at the grave like it had opened a black hole.

"She was sick that whole year," Hayato said. "I mean she'd been sick on and off, but not like this. She had to stop working. She would lie in bed, speaking so low I could barely understand her. She'd hardly eat. We'd have to beg her to take a few bites. Dad had to leave us cash so we could go to the store and make dinner. That's when Subaru started getting his big-brother complex."

"It must've been hard." Of course it had been hard, but what else could Masuo say?

Hayato curled his fingers into a fist. Masuo swallowed, but his mouth remained dry. What kind of boyfriend was he if he couldn't comfort him?

"Then all of us were home for New Year's, and she seemed to perk up," Hayato continued. "She didn't go to the shrine with us or anything, but she ate New Year's food at the table. She even watched a movie after. I thought she was finally getting better. But then Dad had to leave for a three-week-long business trip and school started back. Subaru and I left. She was alone. No one was there to stop her."

The gravity of Hayato's words pressed down on Masuo like a weight. His eyes narrowed. This wasn't the story of a sick mother fighting for her life in a hospital or some freak accident. This was something far worse. Masuo squeezed Hayato's shoulder.

Hayato wet his lips and held on to Masuo's hand even tighter. "We came home from school after that first day back, Subaru unlocked the door, and she was hanging there. A puddle of urine on the floor under her. Subaru tried to block me from seeing. Yelling at me not to look and pushing me out, but I had already seen. I never told him. He got a neighbor to phone our aunt and then the police. They left the door wide open for anyone to see. They didn't care. She was our mother, and they didn't care." Hayato drew in a deep breath, the anguish in his eyes like a knife to Masuo's gut.

"And here I am. I'm her age. I share her blood. I'm predisposed to depression the same way she was. I might do the same thing. What's to stop me? If we hadn't all left her alone, she might still be here." Hayato wiped away the silent tears running down his cheeks.

"I'm sorry." Masuo clutched Hayato's hand, but nothing Masuo could say would make Hayato feel better.

Masuo could only offer a space for Hayato to express his thoughts and offer support so Hayato knew Masuo wouldn't leave.

It took a long while before Hayato spoke again. "I couldn't have come here without you."

Hayato's eyes softened, and a comfortable warmth spread through Masuo's chest. Maybe he hadn't done much, but Hayato's words made him feel a little better.

"Thanks for bringing me here and telling me about her," Masuo said.

Hayato shook his head. "Now you have a good story if someone asks about the worse date you've ever been on."

"No. I would never say that."

"Let's get you back to your grand reopening before you try to convince me this was a good date."

20

Hayato strolled into Masuo's parlor as he closed for the day.

"You're late today," Masuo said.

"I was saving the best for last." Hayato propped the metal briefcase on the prize counter and grinned. "With all that sweet grand reopening money, you can fill me up with your load."

Masuo couldn't hide his chuckle. "Should we head to the back?"

"Hopefully there aren't any big, scary police back there."

Masuo flushed. It was too easy to tease him. "Thanks again for helping out with the reopening when we got back to the city."

Warmth flooded over Hayato. "Well, you helped me this morning. It was only fair I stepped up to help you. I was the reason you were late to your own reopening."

Masuo opened the office door and went to collect the cash.

Hayato uncuffed himself from the briefcase and dug through his inside pocket for a collection of goal coins printed with the parlor's logo. Each in the stack contained the symbol for Masuo's parlor, and such a large stack almost made Hayato worry he'd run out of space in his briefcase.

Masuo came out of the safe closet with two stacks of cash in hand and an even bigger grin across his face. "Not bad, eh?"

Hayato laughed. "Very funny. Now go get the rest."

Masuo's smile faded to a frown. "That's all there was."

"When did you last empty the money machines?"

"An hour ago."

"For the amount of coins here, you should have at least double the cash."

Masuo rubbed the back of his neck, a deep wrinkle marring his brow. "I don't know what to tell you. You can check the safe if you don't believe me."

Hayato didn't need to check. He trusted Masuo, and the man looked like his nerves had been tossed in the fryer. There was no way he was trying to skim off the top.

Hayato grabbed one of the stacks and flipped through the bills. Nowhere near enough, and Endo had taken more interest in Masuo's numbers than any other. Hayato had hoped to bring her a total to prove Masuo knew what he was doing, but the numbers were so low Hayato couldn't hide them under the other parlor totals.

"All the advertising must've attracted a cheater," Hayato said.

Masuo's jaw dropped. "What?"

"It's the only explanation."

"But nothing seemed out of the ordinary."

Hayato squeezed Masuo's shoulder. The little comfort had helped Hayato back at the cemetery; hopefully it would help Masuo now, but he pulled away. Hayato's insides coiled like a snake.

"I can't believe I was stupid enough not to notice."

"The good ones are hard to spot."

"Fuck!" Masuo kicked the edge of his desk, the golden coins scattering.

"Don't stress too much. The cheater probably won't try again for a few days. You're good at setting up plans, so plan for when they come back."

"They'll come back?"

Hayato shrugged. "Maybe. It worked the first time, so they'll probably try again. If they're smart, they'll wait a few days. If they're dumb, they'll come back tomorrow."

Masuo paced the length of the small room, muttering to himself. He'd been able to say the right thing whenever Hayato needed him, but Hayato couldn't do the same for Masuo when the roles were reversed. That alone put Hayato on the horrible boyfriend list.

With so much of his day shrouded in shadows, Hayato couldn't let his grief ruin Masuo's day too. Hayato stepped into Masuo's path and held him by the shoulders. Masuo's muscles coiled tight.

"You're a good businessman," Hayato said. "Today is a cursed day. Keep your eye on people hitting the jackpots tomorrow, and if it feels like they're too lucky, pull the plug and kick them out."

"But what if they're not cheating?"

"It doesn't matter. Too many jackpots are bad for business anyway."

Hopefully the strategy would recoup enough of the

profits that Endo wouldn't request a formal meeting. If it happened again, she'd think one of them was skimming. She'd already made Masuo a target, and it wasn't like she respected Hayato enough that he could convince her it wasn't Masuo's fault.

Masuo's lips flattened into a thin line. "The bastard's going to pay when I catch them."

"On the positive side, this is the biggest load you've brought in. Tomorrow I bet it will be even bigger, right?"

"Yeah..."

"What?" Hayato held a hand to his ear. "I couldn't hear you."

"Right," Masuo said with a bit more enthusiasm.

"That's what I like to hear." Hayato gave Masuo a peck on the cheek. "I gotta get this cash deposited, or they'll think I ran off with it."

Masuo caught Hayato's hand as he turned. "Are you going to be okay? You've had a long day too."

"I'll be fine. My apartment building is doing a new movie club tonight. There's going to be a big crowd."

THE COLD NIGHT surrounded Hayato like the embrace of death, but his smile grew wider the closer he got to his apartment. He'd made it through the day without Subaru's help. The apartment lounge would be packed with people ready to enjoy a film. No one would think it was strange if he showed up and accidentally fell asleep. He probably wouldn't be the only one.

Hayato opened the door to his apartment building and made his way toward the lounge.

"Mr. Kobayashi!"

Hayato ignored the manager and pulled the door handle, but it wouldn't budge. He narrowed his eyes and held his card to the door again. The little light remained red. The manager's heels clacked against the floor.

"Mr. Kobayashi," she repeated, sounding like a schoolteacher scolding the pencil twirlers in the back.

"I'm glad you're here." Hayato smiled. "There seems to be a problem with my card."

She held up one of the orange movie club flyers Hayato had put on all the doors that morning.

"Yes, that's what I'm trying to attend," Hayato said. "A movie club sounds awesome, right? I love movies."

"You put these flyers on every single person's door." She crossed her arms. "How could you think it was the right thing to do after our last conversation?"

Someone was overreacting.

"We had at least a dozen calls about it," she continued.

"So people are interested in the movie club, then?"

"They were calling to complain! This makes strike number three. On top of the complaints, the lease agreement clearly states all formal gatherings in the lounge need proper approval a week in advance."

She held out a piece of paper and pushed it into Hayato's hands. Tiny font peppered the page, but the red eviction notice stood out large at the top.

"You have three days to get out," she said.

"I don't understand."

"You and all your belongings need to vanish within three days, or we'll have to take you to court."

"Fuck this shit." He ripped the paper into pieces.

She pointed to the camera above them. "We have evidence that you received the paperwork should you try to fight it."

"I never wanted to live here anyway."

Hayato threw the pieces of the notice like confetti, then headed to his apartment. Alone.

He was fine.

Everything was fine.

He didn't need the apartment or its stupid lounge.

He opened his suitcase and shoved everything inside. He rubbed his eyes. Subaru didn't need his new life ruined.

He could get through the night without his brother. He could survive. He could make it through one night alone. He was fine by himself.

Until the shadows loomed over him, and his neck grew tight. He coughed, gasping for breath.

He needed to escape.

21

Hayato left his luggage in a train locker and headed to Masuo's apartment. It was on the first floor of a quiet two-story building. Half the exterior lights were out, but the one in front of Masuo's door shined bright, expelling the darkness.

All the relief Hayato needed lay behind that door. He held his breath and knocked. He'd been too scared to call ahead of time. What if Masuo had said no? Then Hayato would have to face the worst night of the year alone.

"Mama!" a muffled voice called.

Hayato narrowed his eyes and doubled-checked the apartment number. The door opened to a little boy dressed in pajamas with a horrible 3D poodle on the front.

"You're not Mama," he said.

No shit, kid.

"Daichi, you shouldn't open the door without an adult." Masuo guided the kid out of the way and raised an eyebrow at Hayato. "Are you okay?"

He plastered on a smile even though it hurt. "You already have kids?"

"They're my neighbor's. She picked up a graveyard shift, so I offered to watch them. Here, come inside. You've got to be freezing."

Hayato hadn't even noticed the cold until he entered the warm apartment. Then a wave of goose bumps pebbled his skin. He took off his shoes and coat.

"Go back to sleep," Masuo told the boy. "Mama won't be here for a while."

"Can I watch *Detective Pom Pom*?"

"*Detective Pom Pom*'s not on in the middle of the night," Masuo said.

"But you have a DVD."

If Hayato had been in a better mood, it might have been cute, but he wasn't, and Daichi's voice sounded like walking into a parlor with all the machines hitting jackpots at once. How was the little girl on the sofa sleeping through it all?

Masuo gave Hayato a faint smile. "Why don't you wait for me in the bedroom. It's that way. I'll just be a second."

Hayato went the way Masuo had pointed. The bedroom was small but neat and orderly like Masuo's expense reports. Hayato sat on the Western-style bed, and his back thanked him. The nights spent on manga café beanbags left it screaming most days. He swallowed and wished he felt less awkward.

"Only one episode and then back to bed," Masuo said, then came into the bedroom.

He opened one of the plastic drawers in the corner and pulled out a tank top, boxers, and a robe. He placed the neatly folded squares beside Hayato.

"You probably want to get out of that stuffy suit."

The *Detective Pom Pom* theme song played. Masuo bounced back into the living room, shutting the door behind him.

Even though Hayato wore underwear, he traded his for Masuo's blue boxers and slipped into the rest of the offerings. Masuo's vanilla-and-oak scent surrounded him. Whatever laundry detergent Masuo used, Hayato needed. Then he could always feel like Masuo was close by.

Hayato pulled back the covers and hugged himself with the ends of the blanket. He wasn't alone anymore. He'd been so lucky to have Masuo.

"You have to keep it low so you don't wake your sister." Masuo's muffled voice came from the living room.

"Okay." Daichi sounded disappointed, but assuming the kid liked Pom Pom as much as Hayato had at his age, Daichi had no doubt already seen the DVD twenty thousand times.

Masuo knocked on the door before creaking it open, then he joined Hayato on the bed and pulled him into his arms.

"Sorry for coming so late." Hayato's voice wouldn't allow him to speak more than a whisper.

"You can come anytime."

"And thanks for the clothes."

"You look pretty hot in them." Masuo pulled the blanket over them. "We should get to sleep."

Hayato pressed his forehead against Masuo's and smiled. This time it didn't hurt. "You don't want to watch Pom Pom?"

Masuo laughed. "I've seen that DVD so many times."

The soft blue light from the crack in the door almost made Masuo glow.

"Thanks." Hayato squeezed Masuo's hand.

"It's not a big deal."

"But it is. Thank you for letting me sleep here and for not asking any questions."

Masuo gave him a knowing smile, but Hayato had to be reading it wrong. People didn't know what monophobia was unless they were the freak who had it.

Then something blurry jumped onto the bed, and Hayato shot up, his heart thumping.

"It's Mochi." Masuo reached out and scratched behind the gray tabby's ear. "Decided you would get more pets in here than sleeping on Sakura's pillow?"

The cat sniffed Hayato's hand for a second before rubbing up against his fingers.

Masuo yawned. "You've got Mochi's approval."

"Or she's angry I'm sleeping in her dad's bed."

"She's not the jealous type."

Hayato lay back down, and Mochi settled on his chest. She was a sturdy cat, but it felt good that, for once, the weight pressing on his chest wasn't fear. He rested a hand in the cat's soft fur, and she purred.

"She's so loud," Hayato said.

"You heard about that study, right?"

"Hmm?"

"The frequency at which cats purr helps promote healing. Mochi wants you to feel better. That's why she's purring."

Hayato closed his eyes. Mochi's purr calmed him and quelled his frantic thoughts, and he finally fell asleep.

HAYATO WOKE up and pulled away from a still sleeping Masuo. Mochi stretched out between their legs. Hayato gave her a good scratch behind the ears, then left the bedroom.

With the children returned to their mother, Hayato was able to get a better view of Masuo's apartment. It was small and a little old. Hayato imagined the grandma who owned it living there since she was a child. She probably even swept the sidewalk each morning. Too bad she didn't have someone to change the light bulbs. It was charming in a way. It wasn't like Hayato owned anything but clothes and accessories. It would be easy to upgrade Masuo's plastic drawers to something with enough room for both of them.

The kitchenette had some rusted burners no doubt older than Masuo, but Hayato wasn't much of a cook, so he didn't mind. He dug through the cabinets, trying to find anything good enough for an asking-to-move-in breakfast. If he wowed Masuo with his pancake skills, he could have his stuff moved in by the end of the day.

There was no way they could squeeze a dining table into such a tiny place. No doubt Subaru and Fumiko would want to come over at some point. Maybe if they got one of those convertible coffee tables that turned into a dining table, it could work. He and Masuo could have that conversation when the time came, but first, the pancakes.

The first one always came out bad, so Hayato hid it under some of the other trash. The second and third slid off the pan perfectly. Masuo didn't have any syrup, so

Hayato made a fresh strawberry-and-whipped-cream topping. Hmm. Maybe they could share in some whipped cream fun before Masuo left for work.

Hayato shimmied out of the clothes Masuo had given him, then he jacked off a little so he'd be at least half hard. The whole point of naked breakfast in bed was the sex, after all.

Hayato took the plates and made his way back into the bedroom. He straddled Masuo's hips, the bulge of his morning wood fitting perfectly behind him. Hayato couldn't wait to experience that pierced cock again.

"It's time to wake up, Masuo," Hayato called, wiggling against him.

"What smells so good?" he asked.

"I made breakfast. Though I'm thinking there is something else I'd rather have."

"Hmm..." Masuo eyed Hayato's half-hard cock. "What would that be?"

"I think you can figure it out."

Their lips met in a soft kiss, but Hayato deepened it. He placed a hand on Masuo's face and used his tongue to explore Masuo's mouth. Hayato could wake up to Masuo's kisses every morning and never get bored.

Masuo pulled back and grabbed a plate. "I don't want breakfast to get cold."

"But this is the last thing on our list."

"We'll have to make a new one." Masuo took a bite of the pancake. "This is yummy."

"Thanks. Pancakes are basically the only thing I'm good at."

"Then you should eat yours too."

Hayato pretended to pout but admitted defeat in

initiating morning sexy time and joined Masuo under the covers.

"Thanks for letting me stay the night," Hayato said.

"Anytime you need it." Even Masuo's bed hair was adorably messy. He cut into one of the pancakes and ate.

As they continued to eat, Masuo explained how he'd met Kira and become her go-to babysitter for her kids. It was sweet. Masuo had a big heart, and that was one of the reasons Hayato loved him. He'd understand how Hayato couldn't live out of a suitcase at a manga café.

"I chatted with Arashi yesterday, and he offered to come and help me watch the parlor." Masuo pushed his last strawberry around in a white pool of deflated cream.

"Two sets of eyes will be good."

"Yeah...I don't want to screw up again in case that cheater comes back."

"You'll be fine."

There was no need to tell Masuo that Endo had examined all Masuo's reports, looking for flaws. Masuo worked so hard he'd be fine. Though he kept pushing around the strawberry like a shark teasing a victim.

Hayato stabbed Masuo's strawberry and ate it. "Come on. Today is a new day. Something amazing could happen."

"Like what?"

"An amazing breakfast. Maybe some hot morning sex?"

"I have to leave in ten minutes."

"A hot morning blow job?"

Masuo wiped a bit of cream off Hayato's lip. "When I get started, I don't want to stop, especially with you."

"Is that supposed to be a compliment or a polite way of turning me down?"

"The more I think about that cheater, the more frustrated I get."

"Okay, no morning sexy time, but today when I come to collect your money, and you rake in tons of profit, we need to do something special to celebrate."

Masuo cracked a smile. "Deal."

Good. Hayato would ask to move in then because nothing would be more special than living with the man he loved.

22

Masuo sat behind the prize counter while Arashi strolled down the row of pachinko machines. A steady stream of customers had come in throughout the day. The numbers might not have been as high as yesterday's grand reopening, but they weren't as low as the week before.

Yesterday's defeat still stung Masuo's pride. The record profits were supposed to have got Endo's attention and proved he wasn't incompetent, but the presence of a cheater had confirmed her first impression of him.

Arashi walked back to the prize counter. "You want to take your lunch? I'll head out after you're finished."

"Yes, please," Masuo said. "I'd love to eat somewhere other than the counter. I always feel like everyone is staring at me and thinking I'm rude."

Arashi had been the best friend Masuo could've asked for. Before opening, they'd brainstormed all the ways someone could've cheated—magnets, wire, somehow getting behind the machine to reprogram it, or some new way they both couldn't figure out. The list made it easier to spot cheats, but so far none of the customers had raised any eyebrows. Masuo couldn't tell if that was something to celebrate or feel more defeated about.

"You going anywhere good?" Arashi asked. "Maybe you can grab me something."

"I'm eating in. Kira made me lunch."

"What?"

"I helped watch her kids last night. It was a thank-you." Masuo grabbed the bento he'd stored behind the counter.

Arashi's mouth dropped open. Then he cleared his throat, trying to hide his surprise. "You should've called. I would've helped out."

"It was short notice."

"Well, next time, call. I don't care about the time."

Masuo laughed. "Okay, any excuse so you can attempt to ask Kira out. Got it."

"She's always so busy. She takes the kids and leaves. I barely get more than a hello in."

"You've gotta say something interesting enough to make her stay for a conversation."

"Can I at least see the bento?"

Masuo laughed and opened the box. Nothing fancy—two rice balls, some miso-glazed chicken, and a hard-boiled egg. Arashi took in a deep breath, inhaling the savory fragrance.

"It looks perfect," Arashi said. "Next time, I'll be sure to make the first move."

MASUO WOULD NEVER GET TIRED of Hayato's long runway walk to the back of the parlor. The way the cuff chain dangled and scratched the metal briefcase conjured up memories of Hayato's arms pulled behind his back and cuffed when they'd screwed in the office. Masuo swallowed. It wasn't anywhere near closing, so he'd have to shut down the erotic trip down memory lane.

Hayato stopped in front of the counter and cocked his hip to the side. "You got enough to fill me up today?"

"I hope so."

Masuo left the door to the office ajar so he could hear the parlor noise. He headed for the safe, while Hayato opened up the briefcase.

"There's something I need to ask you," Hayato said.

Masuo popped open the safe. "What?"

Hayato didn't respond, but it was probably related to the parlor funds. Masuo gathered the cash and the documentation totals. He set the stacks in front of Hayato's open briefcase, trying to judge by the pile of gold coins if the cheater had struck again.

"I got evicted from my apartment," Hayato said. "They found out I was yakuza."

"Oh shit."

Hayato smiled despite the unsettling news. "I had an awesome time with you last night. I was thinking I could move in with you."

"Until you find your own place?"

"I was thinking permanently."

Masuo swallowed and took a step back. A tingling washed over him like he'd banged his funny bone. If only it had been funny. It pushed him off-kilter and changed everything.

"Think about it." Hayato's uncuffed hand wrapped around Masuo's waist. "We'd get to spend the whole night together, and I'm sure we could add a whole lot more to our fantasy list."

Masuo stopped Hayato's hand from traveling to his crotch.

"I love you." Masuo squeezed Hayato's hand. "But we've been together less than a month. It's too soon to talk about living together."

"We get along well. Why wait?"

"If you need to stay for a few days while you find a new place, I'm more than happy to help. But you're talking about forever here."

"Isn't moving in with someone you like the next thing on your relationship to-do list?"

A chasm formed between who Hayato imagined Masuo to be and who he really was. What could he say to make Hayato understand? He took in a breath and spoke from the heart. "When I envisioned moving in with someone, I always expected it to be the person I married."

"Not this again." Hayato rubbed his forehead. "We'll be old men before they legalize same-sex marriage in Japan. Why should we wait to move in together until then? People in America move in together before they're married all the time."

"We're not in America."

"Why are you making this difficult? I have nowhere to live."

"I'm not making it difficult. You can live with me while you look for a new place."

Hayato's hand flexed and closed. He wouldn't look Masuo in the eye.

"It's not that easy for me." Hayato's usually confident tone was flat like a deflated balloon. "I've been trying this whole shitty month, and I failed. Subaru has Fumiko now. He shouldn't have to worry about me anymore."

"I don't understand what you're talking about." Masuo hoped he sounded concerned, but the words were rushed and laced with frustration.

"I'm not right. There's something I should..." Hayato fiddled with the ring on his finger and bit down on his lip. "I'm mono—"

Hayato's phone rang, cutting him off. The ringtone was a death march.

"Ward Leader Endo," Hayato answered.

"How much did he make today?" Her voice was loud enough for Masuo to hear.

Hayato shuffled around the stack of cash. Masuo's pulse pounded louder than a pachinko machine. For Hayato to know exactly what Endo was talking about, they must've been discussing the parlor's totals regularly. Masuo rubbed his palm against his pants, and Hayato read the total listed on the document sheet.

"That doesn't seem like much, all things considered," Endo said.

Hayato turned away from Masuo. "Sure, it's a little light, but maybe a few people got lucky. It usually wouldn't raise an eyebrow."

"But so many days in a row?"

"Maybe we can give him another day. The place was a real shithole before. It'll take a bit for word to get out."

"We'll have a meeting tomorrow at four. Fill the idiot in on the details. Make sure he gets there on time."

Hayato hung up.

"Damn it." Masuo slammed his fist against the table. "Arashi and I made a game plan, and we watched everyone. I can't believe it. How could a cheater have snuck their way in?"

Hayato's shoulders slumped, and he locked the briefcase silently. It took a moment for Masuo's brain to catch up. His heart didn't know where to focus his worry —on Hayato or the parlor.

"What were you saying before she called?" Masuo asked.

"Forget it. In fact, forget everything. All of it." Hayato's words stabbed like a knife to the gut.

"I..." Masuo bit his lip. "You can tell me."

"Make sure you get to the safe house on time."

Hayato stalked off, and Masuo knew he'd fucked up.

23

The last thing Hayato wanted to do was knock on Subaru's door, but his brother would be more suspicious if he'd called off their weekly meal. Hayato's lower back twinged from another night's sleep on the manga café's beanbag. The solitude would swallow him whole if he stayed at a normal hotel. He put on a happy face and knocked on the door.

Fumiko answered in a dress better suited for spring than winter, but her sunny disposition warmed the coldest day.

"Come on in," she said. "The oden stew is almost finished."

"Oh, wow, you two must've been cooking all morning."

"My family always makes it the night before."

"That sounds easier."

"And it allows the fish cakes to soak up more of the flavor. So today we're only reheating."

The deep savory aroma of fish and daikon hit Hayato. "It smells delicious."

A few more touches of Fumiko's style decorated the small apartment. A vase of fresh flowers on a side table and a rolling closet full of dresses. Fumiko worked for an indie brand specializing in vintage American clothing and reproductions.

"They're from the new line at work," Fumiko said. "The boss wants to make sure I get pictures wearing them for the store's social media page."

"Must be nice to get an updated wardrobe each season."

"Not when there's barely enough room for Subaru's suits in the closet."

So the honeymoon phase was over.

Subaru had gotten the same bump in salary after the safe-house massacre. He could afford a place with more storage. No doubt he'd been socking the money away for his life with Fumiko.

"You look tired." Subaru handed Hayato one of Fumiko's cocktails.

"I'm fine." Hayato took a sip and puckered his lips at the lemony drink. Then he continued, knowing "fine" wasn't going to satisfy Subaru for very long. "I have a meeting with Endo after this."

"What happened?"

"A cheater has hit one of the parlors two days in a row. It's looking bad. Now Endo wants a meeting with me and the manager. Is the oden finished? I'm so hungry I could eat the whole pot."

Hayato's stomach might've been empty, but not as much as his heart. It would've been easier if he'd actually resolved his fight with Masuo. Why couldn't they live together to see if they matched first? Subaru and Fumiko lived together and weren't married. So it wasn't the traditional thing. Who cared?

Subaru brought a large earthenware pot to the dining table. Hayato had never seen it before, so it must be Fumiko's. She lifted the lid, and steam rolled off the stew. Daikon, octopus, and aburaage lay on top of dashi. Hayato's stomach rumbled.

Fumiko chuckled.

"I've been waiting all day for this." Hayato patted his stomach, hitting the ball of his navel piercing.

They dug in to the stew. Hayato attacked the deep-fried tofu pouches with mochi inside. He took a bite, leaned back, and closed his eyes. If Fumiko always cooked such delicious meals, maybe he could convince Subaru they should all live together or at least buy a house and let Hayato sleep in the shed.

"We're eating at your place next week, right?" Subaru asked, but it was more of a demand.

Hayato laughed. "I don't have a table yet."

"Doesn't it get awkward when you eat?"

"I usually eat out."

Subaru's gaze lay into Hayato like a lecture. Of course he'd figured Hayato out. He always knew everything. Hayato looked backed to his stew and pushed a flower-cut carrot around in his bowl. He needed to throw off Subaru's suspicion before his stare made Hayato confess everything.

"This is such a nice dinner. It helped to get my mind off the cheater." Hayato tried to read Subaru's face but got nothing. "They were supposed to give us cushy jobs after everything we went through, but here I am worried about profit margins."

"Every job has its ups and downs," Fumiko said. "The store doesn't pay super well, but it lets me get off for competitions."

Hayato nodded, though getting shot at by the Korean mob was a bit of an extreme downside.

The excuse seemed to work enough for Subaru, who finally went back to enjoying his meal. They chatted a little about their upcoming competition.

"The other day I saw they redid *Detective Pom Pom*." Hayato grabbed another daikon from the pot. "But he's 3D now and bad looking. It's like they tainted my childhood."

Fumiko laughed. "The other day, Subaru and I went to the rental store and brought home the Detective Pom Pom movie."

The daikon dropped out of Hayato's chopsticks. "What?"

Subaru shrugged. "Why not?"

"With how often we watched it as kids, you could've recited it from memory."

"He did quote a few lines," Fumiko said.

Hayato laughed. "Our parents had to buy double of everything when it came to the detective because we once got into a big fight about who got to sleep with the one Pom Pom plushie they'd bought us. It was bad. Subaru ended up with seven stitches."

Fumiko's eyes widened.

"Hayato shoved me," Subaru said. "I slipped and landed on the side of our metal train set."

The brothers shared a few more stories, and the level

of the stew in the pot sunk more and more. Strangely, Fumiko had somehow made it through childhood without obsessing over the poodle detective.

Once she finished her meal, she kissed Subaru's cheek. "I need to get going to work, honey cake." Fumiko nodded to Hayato. "Next week we're going to your place."

Hayato held up his hands. "Don't expect something as good as this. I'm good at pancakes."

"Pancakes for dinner. We can watch Pom Pom and pretend we're kids again."

She grabbed her bag and left, and the door shut behind her.

"What's going on?" Subaru asked.

Hayato sank back in his chair. Where to start? The eviction because he couldn't stay the night alone or the horrible argument with Masuo that left their relationship a huge question mark?

Hayato couldn't talk about his monophobia. Subaru had finally begun his happy life with Fumiko. Hayato couldn't throw his needs into their happy relationship. Hayato had to learn to be alone at some point. Maybe being thrown into the deep end was what he needed. So far, though, he'd sunk like his shoes were made of concrete.

"The manager in trouble is Masuo, right?" Subaru leaned forward.

At least he'd picked the topic for them.

Hayato nodded. "We got into a big fight. I said some stupid stuff and kind of messed everything up."

It was a half truth, but it was close enough that Subaru's big-brother powers probably wouldn't sniff it out.

"Everyone messes up," Subaru said. "It's part of relationship building. Apologize and move on."

"You make it sound so easy."

"If you mean your apology and care about each other, you'll figure it out."

Hayato and his exes had never done the whole apologize-and-move-on thing. Usually it either ended the relationship right away or they ignored the issue so it festered and burst later.

Subaru exposed all Hayato's weaknesses. How had he ended up such a helpless mess when his twin faced every situation with resilience?

"Fumiko and I have had a few big arguments," Subaru confessed. "Even a few since she moved in."

"Really?"

"Mostly about whether we should break the lease and move someplace bigger. It's a relationship, and two people don't necessarily always agree on everything."

Hayato's throat went dry. He hadn't allowed Masuo the time to explain himself. Why had Hayato walked out on such a good thing?

Hayato rubbed his face. "I fucked up."

"Everyone does. Try to smooth things over before the meeting with Endo. Give both of you the space and time to talk. That won't be too hard, right?"

Subaru always made everything sound so easy.

"I could probably call, and we could figure things out."

"Good, you made a plan. Now there's something I want to ask you. You can say no, and that's fine."

Hayato narrowed his eyes. Nothing good could come from a start like that. "What?"

"Remember when you said if I ever found a woman I wanted to marry that you'd be willing to give me our mother's ring? Well, I want to propose to Fumiko."

The host family Mom had stayed with in the US had had a ring that was passed down in their family for three generations. Their mother would always go on about how romantic the idea was and told them she'd be happy to give up her ring to whichever of us found a woman willing to wear it. It wasn't exactly the most common practice in Japan, but they'd both grown up with the story.

"You're not afraid Fumiko's going to think there's some horrible curse attached to it, since Mother was wearing it when she killed herself?" Hayato sounded bitter, but he wasn't.

He wasn't. He'd known the day would come.

"Fumiko and I talked about it when we visited Mom's grave." Subaru smiled. "I told her the same story Mom used to tell us about seeing the ring in the photographs of their great-great-grandmother."

"I remember. Her whole face would light up, and she'd say how it was the most romantic thing in the world. Then she'd want to watch rom-coms for the rest of the day."

Hayato rubbed the tears out of his eyes before they could fall. Sometimes even the happy memories hurt because no matter how much their mother had smiled, there had been so many days she hadn't. She had had a disease, and it had eaten her alive. But they couldn't talk about it. It wasn't the same as if it had been a car crash or cancer. They'd had to keep the cause of her death quiet because of societal stigma that would bleed out and cover them as well.

"It hurts." Hayato's voice shook. "Why couldn't everything have been different?"

"I know." Subaru's sigh carried the same weight Hayato bared. "It's a hard month on top of a hard year. That's why I rented the Detective Pom Pom movie. I always do in January to remember the happy memories and when Mom got to be who she was meant to be. This year, I got to watch it with Fumiko. While we were watching, I realized she's the one I always want to be with. I know you wear Mom's ring, and if you don't want to give it to me, it's fine."

Hayato slid off the ring and put it in Subaru's hand. "If it goes to Fumiko, then I have no problem handing it over. I know she'll make an awesome sister-in-law."

"Thanks." Subaru smiled. "I know you'll figure out things with Masuo."

"I hope so."

24

The Kyoto yakuza insignia had been taken down from the Fushimi ward headquarters after the Korean mob had used it for target practice. Without it, the building looked like any other office building. But looking at it still made Masuo's mouth go dry. He'd spent all night planning how he'd earn the right to keep his parlor.

He checked his paperwork one last time and knocked on the door. Entering, Masuo locked eyes with the two dead black voids of the glued-together Mayumaro figure. The cocooned silkworm mocked him. Usually it was kept high up on a shelf, but Endo had probably had it moved just for him.

"Endo wants you to wait outside her office," the recruit said.

Hayato already stood outside Endo's office. His suit was pressed, and his golden, bronze hair was unstyled and straight as hay. Even the sheen of his lip gloss was gone. He looked up when Masuo stood beside him.

"I tried to call you." Hayato kept his voice low.

"I know," Masuo said.

"You didn't answer."

"Because I was mad at you. I still am. You wouldn't even hear me out. Then you tell me to forget about it like nothing happened? How am I supposed to take that? Are you going to get mad and leave any time we disagree about something?"

"I'm going to make it up to you. I promise. You'll see." Hayato reached out toward Masuo, but he stepped out of reach.

"I don't need help. I got it all figured out here." Masuo held up the papers.

Endo's door opened. One of the street captains shuffled out, his forehead creased with worry.

"You two get in here," Endo said.

Her short blond hair stuck out every which way. She was in her forties but had never lost the girl-gang-biker death glare. Every man in the Fushimi ward knew she could kick their asses, and she kept an iron-fisted grip on her power.

They both give a low bow. "Ward Leader Endo."

"Sit." Her tone was as sharp as a knife.

Hayato sat in the leather chair directly in front of her, while Masuo ended up in one behind him. The office was minimal and contained furniture made from steel, wood, and leather. The only decorative piece was the picture of Father Murata behind Endo. If Endo's stare wasn't enough to scare the shit out of Masuo, then Murata's was. Even in the photograph, his glare ignited a visceral wave of fear in Masuo.

Endo tapped the ash off her cigarette and let it rest

between her fingers. "Looks like money hasn't been good the past few days."

"I—"

She held up her hand. "Who gave you permission to speak?"

Masuo bowed his head and mumbled an apology. He'd been so eager to show his work he'd forgotten standard protocol.

"Your grand reopening scheme was supposed to pull in the money, right?" she asked, but it wasn't a question. "This little jump in sales is pitiful. Especially when compared to the amount your parlor had to pay out. What do you have to say for yourself?"

Endo handed Masuo the rope to hang himself, and Hayato just sat there the whole time, his face cast down, as if too ashamed to speak.

Masuo swallowed. "The past two days, there's been a suspected cheater. I've been trying to catch them. I have some projections if we ignore it and go with the average—"

"It's clear running a parlor isn't for you."

"If you look at the percentage profits over the course of the weeks before—"

Endo held up her hand to silence him. Cigarette smoke swirled around her.

"You spent all this money on an opening and even bought new machines, and it still fails. I don't care about the percentage profits. What kind of yakuza lets a cheater get away unscathed? Especially one bold enough to return twice." Endo shook her head. "Someone with more experience would have had that cheater on their knees. You can be a janitor at one of the other parlors and learn a few things."

Masuo's hands twisted into fists. Everything he'd worked for. His dream of turning the parlor around and finally proving himself. Endo had already made up her mind. She wouldn't even allow Masuo to defend himself, but he wouldn't let it slip through his fingers without a fight.

"I've made several projections." Masuo held out the first paper to back up his claims. "If you look here, you can see—"

Hayato cleared his throat. "Part of this is my fault."

Endo stubbed out her cigarette. "Really? How?"

"I never took the time to show Masuo the ropes."

Masuo's heart dropped to his gut. He hadn't asked Hayato to do anything to help. Maybe he meant well, but it only caused the storm within Masuo to rage. He wanted to save himself, not be rescued.

Endo tapped her nails on the desk. "Maybe they did things differently in Yamashita, but here I expect my men to do their jobs."

"It's not a good excuse, but it is what it is."

How dare Hayato try to say Masuo was so incompetent he couldn't run a business without Hayato walking him through it.

"You think because you survived an attack you'll have it easy for the rest of your time with the family? I think not." Endo crossed her arms. "You need to get your act together. The Korean mafia isn't done with us. Everyone knows that. Where do you think the pachinko money goes? Clearly you need to spend some more time training the managers." Endo looked at Masuo. "What time do you open?"

"Ten."

"For the next week, Hayato will be with you from open to close. That'll give him enough time to show you how to run a parlor. No more mistakes for a week, and you can keep the parlor." She glanced back to Hayato. "After that week, you'll do the same for every single parlor in the ward."

Hayato nodded. "I understand."

Endo snapped her fingers to get Masuo's attention. "You've got a week to straighten up your parlor or else it's going to someone else. Get to work."

Masuo left, and Hayato followed. He yammered on about something, but Masuo couldn't quiet his rage. Once they got out of sight of any of the windows, Masuo threw his collection of papers in front of Hayato.

"I was supposed to earn my stay at the parlor, not have you admit you showed me nothing!" The release of the bitter words felt sweet to Masuo. "I could've handled myself in there. I didn't need your help."

Hayato pressed his lips together, finally shutting up for once. "But it's true. I didn't train you like I was supposed to, so it's my fault. I wanted to take the blame because I knew she'd give me a second chance. You? I'm not so sure."

"You can be such a self-absorbed dick."

"This month is hard for me."

"What's your excuse for the other eleven? You can't be the biggest jerk in the world one month and a saint the rest."

"Masuo..."

"I don't need your help. I need to earn the right to keep the parlor on my own."

Masuo ran away before Hayato could say anything else because he didn't want to hear it. Whatever excuse Hayato would conjure would only distract Masuo from doing his job.

25

Hayato slept more at the manga café than he ever had at his apartment. He might as well call the space with the drop ceiling with the mysterious stains home.

He popped his shoulder, hoping it would help his aching muscles. It didn't. He sighed and let the manga drop from his hands. He'd screwed things up with Masuo —*again*—and now they'd be stuck together in the world's smallest pachinko parlor for twelve hours a day every day for a week.

How could Hayato have been so careless? Masuo had started to fight for his parlor by presenting evidence of his managerial skills, and Hayato had opened his big mouth. It was like he'd never paid attention to Masuo. Of course Masuo wanted to earn the right to keep his parlor. Hayato should have kept his big mouth closed. He should've waited and allowed Masuo to try before sweeping in and solving the problem.

Hayato's alarm sounded, signaling he needed to get to

the parlor. He heaved himself up from the beanbag, but his foot cramped. He reached out and braced himself against one of the flimsy temporary walls, but his foot caught underneath the beanbag.

"Fuck!"

The beanbag flipped. The tape holding a ripped seam tore open. Millions of tiny Styrofoam balls exploded out like blood gushing from a cut to the jugular. The balls coordinated their attack on Hayato. They stuck to everything. Hayato's suit, jacket, face. He tried to brush them off, but then they only stuck to more places.

He looked like an idiot pretending to be a snowman. He left the room and the manga café, shedding a few of the balls with each step, but with so many clinging to him, it was hardly noticeable.

People who dared to get too close to Hayato on the train left with a few balls stuck to them. Hayato had set his alarm early, since he'd figured Masuo would get to the parlor early, but the door was locked when Hayato arrived.

Hayato paced as he waited, imagining all the different scenarios for his morning with Masuo. Maybe he'd forgive Hayato and realize he'd only meant to help, or maybe he'd refuse to even let Hayato in.

Hayato turned and spotted Masuo coming down the street, his arms crossed.

"What are you doing here?" Masuo's tone was more bitter than an unripe persimmon.

"I have to follow Endo's orders."

"Weren't you the one who told me I exceeded all your expectations? What could you show me that I don't already know?"

Hayato bit his lip. It was true.

"Think of me as an extra hand. You can practice for when you get an extra worker once your parlor makes bank." Hayato winked, but Masuo rolled his eyes, annoyed.

He opened the gate and headed to his office. Hayato followed.

"What do I need to do first?" Hayato leaned against the doorframe. "You're the boss. Order me around. Your wish is my command."

Masuo didn't speak, but his shoulders stiffened with Hayato's words. Their gazes met for a second.

Then Masuo pulled out a thick envelope from his pocket and pushed it toward Hayato. "This is for you."

Hayato snatched the envelope and opened it. "What's all this cash for?"

"It's for the machines. I don't want to owe you anything."

The words stung. Hayato opened his mouth, but nothing came out.

Masuo ripped out a page from his notebook. "And here's everything I want you to do before we open. We need to rush, since I had to close early for the meeting yesterday."

"Where did you even get all this money?" Hayato said.

"My savings. The rest I borrowed from Arashi."

"Wait. Let's talk about this."

"Hurry up and get to the list."

How was Hayato supposed to fix their relationship if Masuo was stubbornly refusing to talk? Hayato ground his teeth together and swallowed the urge to rip Masuo's list into tiny pieces to match the Styrofoam balls still stuck to his coat.

Subaru had said relationships took work. And while saying "fuck it" to Masuo would've been easy, when Hayato thought about his future, he envisioned Masuo by his side. Hayato counted the money and took out a few extra notes.

"You gave me too much." Hayato put the extra few bills aside.

"It's the interest."

Hayato pressed a hand over his chest as if trying to stop the bleeding. His heart pounded like he was back in the safe house, the Korean mob climbing up the stairs, but instead of fighting for his life, Hayato was fighting for Masuo.

"You're right," Hayato said. "I can be a jerk and self-absorbed and an asshole."

"I never called you an asshole."

"Well, it's true. You've always been honest with me, and I've..." Hayato bit his bottom lip. "I've been holding something back that you should've known a while ago."

Masuo leaned in his squeaky office chair. He raised an eyebrow but didn't say anything.

"I have monophobia. I've had it since I was young. Since that day." Hayato took a breath, searching Masuo's face for any sign of hope, but he only tilted his head. "I'm afraid to be alone. It was years before I noticed, and it's gotten worse over time. When I'm alone, my throat starts to close. I can't breathe. My thoughts race thinking about my mother. She had been fine before we'd left for school, and she wouldn't have done it if we were there. My thoughts jump, and I can't separate myself from her. What's stopping me from doing the same thing?"

"Hayato..."

"I promise this is going somewhere."

"We'll have people in here in twenty minutes."

"Please." Hayato's voice shook with desperation. "It's important to me that you know."

Masuo sighed. "Make it quick."

"When you said I was self-absorbed, I was confused. How could I be self-absorbed when I'm constantly thinking about how to keep people around me? But now I see. I only worried about myself. I'm not perfect, far from it, but I'm trying to be better. You're the reason I'm trying to be better. Maybe if we work together, we can help each other." Hayato closed his eyes, fearing the worst. "I want you to be the best pachinko parlor manager, the best businessman, the best Masuo you can be. Maybe it's selfish again to want to be the one to help you, but I'm here."

"Okay."

Hayato bit his lip. "And I'm sorry for blowing up when you said I couldn't move in. It's fine that you want to wait to be married before you move in with someone. I might not get it, but I'll honor your wishes and not bring it up again."

A small smile crept onto Masuo's face. It wasn't the big overjoyed reaction Hayato had fantasized about, but it was progress.

"So I'll just get to the things on the list." Hayato reached out to take the paper, but Masuo pulled it out of his reach.

"And maybe it was wrong to get so upset when you were only helping."

Hayato nodded. "You more than earned your spot as parlor manager. It's probably going to be years before Endo says it. I've been in this ward for months, and you saw how she treated me."

"And you're basically a war hero."

"That's a good joke."

Masuo pointed to Hayato's sleeve of white balls. "Now, why do you look like a crazy person?"

Hayato pressed his lips together. "There was an accident. It's nothing to worry about."

"The customers won't appreciate you looking like you got into a fight with a shipping box. Get over here." Masuo dug through the drawer and pulled out a lint brush.

"I thought Mochi's cat hair was a reminder of your sweet kitty," Hayato said, hoping the joke landed.

Masuo cracked a smile and handed Hayato the brush. "She doesn't need to be with me everywhere."

Hayato rolled up the balls on the sticky sheet. It took five passes, one for each limb and one for his body. He exchanged the brush for the list and headed out.

"Wait," Masuo laughed. "It's all over your back."

He grabbed Hayato's elbow and turned him around so he could get the back of his jacket.

"Thanks," Hayato said.

Masuo cleared his throat. "We had our first fight."

"If we don't count the little fight over the fantasy list, then it was the first one."

"Ah, that's right." Masuo turned to face Hayato. "You

know, I like to make lists and keep to the plans I've envisioned."

Hayato held up the list in his hand. "Very detailed lists."

"Well, number one on my 'how to maintain a healthy relationship after a fight' list is to kiss and make up."

"Hmm...I don't see that on my list."

Masuo laughed.

Hayato grabbed a pen off the desk and began to write "kiss and make up" across the top of the list he held, but Masuo wouldn't let him finish. He pulled Hayato into a warm embrace and kissed him. It was the kind of kiss that smoothed away any worries or lingering doubts that they wouldn't last. They'd make it together, and Hayato would do whatever he could to make Masuo's parlor a success.

26

Masuo sat behind the prize counter. The parlor closed in half an hour, and the only people there were he and Hayato. So of course Hayato strolled over with a mischievous grin.

"Want to catch a movie after I get off?" Hayato asked.

Masuo shrugged. "I think we've seen everything that's out already."

"Then I'm sure we can find something fun to do."

"Maybe we can go once we catch the cheater. It can be a reward."

"The cheater hasn't shown their face in six days. Your profits have been so good that Endo's going to let you keep the parlor. Isn't that enough to celebrate?"

"I'd feel better telling Endo I caught the bastard."

Hayato's chipper attitude the past week had lifted Masuo's spirits, but even with the bigger profits, knowing the cheater had gotten off without punishment pissed him off. The cheater deserved to get caught.

"Hey now, what's with that face? Do I need to drag you to the back and cheer you up?"

Masuo cracked a smile. "I'm fine."

"If you change your mind, I get off in half an hour." Hayato winked.

A man stumbled into the parlor. He must've recently finished a drunken meal with his coworkers. He fumbled with his wallet before exchanging his cash for a tub of balls and hit one of the machines.

"Hopefully this one doesn't puke," Hayato mumbled.

"Go by the entry. I don't like the look of this," Masuo said, though he didn't like the look of most of the customers.

"Whatever you say, boss."

By the time Hayato meandered to the other side of the parlor, the customer had hit his first jackpot. The machine got louder, the lights flashed, and the next boobtastic villain popped up on the LCD screen for the vampire hunter to defeat. Masuo narrowed his eyes. It was possible to get lucky, but it had still been a fast win.

Hayato tried to look busy cleaning the machines while he watched the man. The machine got louder again, thumping out the next level of double payout as Booberella got impaled by a very suggestive spear. The guy reached into his pocket and tapped out a cigarette like a double jackpot was nothing.

The man played the machine like an instrument, but even under Masuo's scrutiny, he couldn't detect anything out of the ordinary.

Hayato finished cleaning the row of machines, then squatted to clean the front of the display case.

"I think the guy has a wire or something," Hayato

said, not looking up at Masuo. "He's already hit two jackpots, and the new machines are set to have slower payouts."

Masuo pulled out a piece of paper. "Let's list all the possible next steps, then we can make a plan."

"Part of being a good yakuza is trusting your gut. Like with the yakuza who rescued you from the elevator. I'm sure it wasn't on his to-do list, but did he think twice about saving you? No. This guy is probably cheating, so we should kick his ass."

The grid lines of the paper called to Masuo to fill them with a detailed list of plans, but Hayato had a point. Sometimes lists got in the way and didn't help. Masuo had had a detailed plan for how to save his parlor, one that Endo would've most likely rejected, but Hayato had used his gut and stepped in to help.

Masuo pushed the paper aside. "Go clean the other row of machines. Get ahead of him. Then, when I nod my head, I'll reach for him from the back, and you get him from the front. If we confront him on both sides, he'll probably go quietly."

Hayato smiled and went back to cleaning. Masuo's foot bounced at the edge of his stool before Hayato shot him a cut-it-out look that caught Masuo's breath. He couldn't give off any hint that he suspected the guy was a cheating bastard.

Masuo organized the already pristine prize collection while he waited for Hayato to make his way to clean the machines on the other side of the cheater. Masuo nodded, and they both leisurely shuffled toward the man.

Hayato took an empty ball tub and passed them to the cheater. "Here's another one for you, sir."

While the man was distracted, Masuo grabbed his arm. A thin, almost invisible wire came out of his sleeve. The man used all his weight to shove Masuo to the ground, then tripped Hayato flat on his ass. The cheater ran out. All the stumbling about like a drunkard gone. It had all been an act.

"I'll lock up and then catch up with you," Hayato said.

Masuo jumped to his feet and gave chase. The cheater zigzagged this way and that, knocking over signboards and store displays as he went.

Masuo's heart pounded in his ears. He could see the fate of the parlor resting before him. He wouldn't let victory slip away.

Hayato caught up to them, and having him close gave Masuo a second burst of adrenaline.

The cheater ran into a hotel.

"I'll follow him inside. You see if he heads out a back entrance," Masuo said more on instinct than working from any thought-out plan.

Hayato split off, while Masuo remained on the cheater's heels.

The after-dinner crowd congregated outside the hotel's restaurant, but they scattered as the cheater cut through them, leaving a path for Masuo to follow. The man headed toward the back and to a large set of windows and doors. A small nook held a pay phone, while the open nook next to it held a decorative plant.

Hayato emerged in front of the door, blocking the man's exit. He doubled back and dove inside the small paneled room.

A wicked grin crossed Masuo's face. They had the bastard cornered.

"I wasn't doing anything," the cheater pleaded.

Masuo pulled back his fist, aiming to land a jab square on the bastard's jaw.

Ding.

Everything turned white, and horror struck Masuo like a ball tossed about in the pins of a pachinko machine. He held his breath and glanced over his shoulder. A set of paneled doors closed tight, and the room gave the distinct lurch of an elevator springing to life.

"Fuck."

The air left his lungs, and Masuo's legs went weak. He was trapped in an elevator and couldn't escape.

The cheater lunged at Masuo and knocked the last of his air out of him. They tumbled to the ground. Masuo kicked the cheater in the face. Blood spurted from his nose.

"You think you can steal from my parlor?" Masuo grabbed the plant and slammed it on the cheater's head.

The cheater went limp, but his chest still rose with his breath. He'd live but would think twice about coming into Masuo's parlor ever again. He pulled out the man's wallet and took the cash.

"You show your face at my parlor again, and you're dead," Masuo warned.

The cheater mumbled an agreement.

Another lurch and the elevator stopped. The doors opened, and Hayato stood outside with his hands on his knees, panting.

"You...did it," he said around gulps of air.

Masuo stepped out of the elevator, and it was like coming out of a fantasy world. He could finally feel his heart pounding again. Somehow, he'd managed to go into the steel death trap. The victory over the cheater mixed with the euphoria of stepping into an elevator made Masuo's blood rush. Masuo's hands wrapped around Hayato's waist and pulled him in for a kiss.

The elevator dinged, sending the cheater away.

Masuo smiled and interlaced his fingers with Hayato's.

"Should we celebrate?" Masuo asked. "Maybe we could skip the movie and get a room at the hotel. It would be an upgrade from our previous room with the fuzzy heart-shaped pink bed."

Hayato's tongue darted out to wet his lips, but it wasn't done in a sultry, come-hither way.

"I can't tell you how much I want to say yes." Hayato's voice came out strained and like he was second-guessing every word that came from his glossed lips. "But all month I've been trying to make it on my own one full night, and I keep screwing up. If you can get into an elevator, then I should be able to sleep in a room where I can't hear the person next to me."

"You don't have to push yourself because of me."

"I don't want to be a burden to my brother or to you. Once I do this, I promise we'll have the most amazing night ever."

Masuo laughed. "Okay. Why don't you call me when you're getting ready for bed?"

Hayato narrowed his eyes. "Isn't that cheating?"

"One of my high school girlfriends always made sure we called each other before bed. Sometimes she would even nod off to sleep while we were on the phone. Don't you get to decide your own definition of what being alone means? So decide talking on the phone until you fall asleep still counts."

"Okay. I'll call you before I go to sleep."

"I know you can do it. Masuo squeezed Hayato's hands and hoped the extra affection would help him conquer his fear.

27

H ayato swallowed hard, pushing back his fear of spending the night alone, and entered the video rental store. It was well into the night, but a half dozen other customers still lingered inside. He had to do it at some point. He needed to give it a decent try.

"Is there something specific you're looking for?" one of the employees asked.

"Do you have the Detective Pom Pom movie?" Hayato asked.

"Ah, the kids are having trouble sleeping, eh?"

Hayato rubbed his neck. "Yeah..."

"The detective puts mine right to sleep. The kids' section is this way."

The worker led Hayato to a rack that had been dedicated to the show.

The man pulled out one of the boxes and handed it to Hayato, but the cover had a picture of the horrible 3D Pom Pom.

"Do you have the older version?"

The man laughed. "Of course. I always preferred the hand-drawn look myself."

Hayato took the older movie, then grabbed a few other DVDs from another section so it wouldn't look odd when he checked out.

With the movies secured, Hayato grabbed his bag from the train station locker and checked in to a nice hotel. There were dozens of hotels to pick from, but Hayato picked one with the nicest-looking bathroom. Spending two weeks washing up in a tiny stall had made him crave the luxury of a deep soak in a bath.

He leaned against the back wall of the hotel elevator and stared at himself in the warped golden walls. If Masuo could go into an elevator, nothing would stop Hayato from staying the night alone. He'd been working on it all month, albeit mostly failing, but with Masuo's words echoing in his heart, it finally felt possible.

Hayato entered the Western-style room. A huge fluffy bed greeted him. He flung himself onto it and sank into the plush comforter. All the little aches and pains from the nights on the stupid beanbags melted away.

It was already after eleven. If he could actually fall asleep and stay asleep for six hours, he'd call it a success.

But it didn't take long for the silence to sink in.

He was alone.

No one was there to stop him from doing something stupid and ending up like his mother.

Hayato swallowed the rising panic in his throat and touched the phone in his pocket. Masuo was a phone call away. He expected Hayato at the parlor tomorrow morning. If Hayato didn't show up, Masuo would be worried and go looking for him.

And Masuo expected a call tonight.

Hayato's muscles loosened, and he took in a deep breath. He could make it through the night.

He popped the Pom Pom DVD into the player. The familiar opening images of the animated poodle caused a wave of memories to wash over Hayato. He and Subaru had watched it so many times they'd memorized it. They would take turns playing Pom Pom and act out the lines for fun. Their parents must've hated the movie by the time they'd grown out of the phase.

Hayato crawled under the covers and called Masuo.

"Sorry it's so late," Hayato said. "I had to drop off the cash at the safe house, then go over the details with Endo. Everything took longer than I thought it would."

"Oh?"

"I told her all about the impressive way you took down the cheater. I even dropped a hint about how your profits seem to be matching the trajectory information you gave her, then suggested that if your projections continue to match over the next month, you should get a part-time worker to help you out."

"Not a day off?" Masuo joked.

"I might have to lick her shoes before she even takes my part-timer suggestion. You deserve it though."

Masuo chuckled, his voice sleepy. Hayato hated that he had to call him so late.

"Calling you still feels like cheating," Hayato said.

"Would it be better if I called you?"

"I..." Hayato bit his lip. "Maybe?"

Masuo hung up and a few seconds later called back.

"Ah, Hayato, thanks for answering," Masuo said. "I'm

having trouble sleeping. You mind talking to me for a little while?"

Hayato's heart soared at the words. What magic had he somehow conjured to get Masuo to stick around?

"Sure," Hayato said. "I sometimes have trouble falling asleep too."

"Are you watching TV?"

"I'm watching the Detective Pom Pom movie."

Masuo laughed. "Pom Pom is number one."

Hayato snuggled a little deeper into the bed. "Is Mochi with you?"

"Taking up half my pillow."

"Hmm," Hayato yawned. "She's queen of the house."

"Can you hear her purring? I think she's doing it because she can hear you on the other end of the line."

Mochi's purring grew louder. Hayato closed his eyes, imagining the night she'd lain on his chest and Masuo had held on to his hand. It had been so peaceful. It was almost like he was back there.

"Hayato?" Masuo's voice sounded quiet and far away.

"Hmm."

"I love you."

"I love you too."

With Mochi's steady purr in his ear and Masuo's words in his heart, Hayato found sleep.

HAYATO'S ALARM cut through his dream. The intro animation for the Pom Pom DVD kept playing the first few lines of the theme song before instructing the user to press play. He clicked off the TV, then snuggled deeper into his blanket cocoon. He wanted to sleep.

He drifted off...

The alarm went off again five minutes later. Hayato groaned and turned it off correctly but then noticed the time.

Eight?

He'd managed to sleep through the whole night. By himself!

A whole night of restful sleep. All because Masuo's voice had been the last thing he'd heard.

He thumbed through his contacts, ready to call Masuo to scream in celebration, but he realized Masuo would be getting ready for work too.

Hayato washed up and got dressed quicker than he ever had. He extended his stay at the hotel for the rest of the week and made a quick stop at a café. He bought a few celebration-worthy treats and arrived at the parlor gate at the same time as Masuo.

Hayato handed Masuo a cup. "I got you a coffee."

"You didn't have to."

Hayato held up his cup.

"Are we toasting?" Masuo asked.

"Yes, to your victory over elevators and my night alone."

Masuo's eyes widened. "You did it?"

"I have you to thank for it." Hayato's voice caught in the back of his throat. "I know one night is only the beginning, and I have a long way to go, and I was talking with—"

Masuo's kiss cut off Hayato's words. It was deep and filled with every bit of longing Hayato had held back all morning. It was a kiss Hayato felt down to his toes. He dropped his coffee and clutched onto Masuo, hoping to convey his deep-seated need to be with him because Hayato knew he would never find the words to express it.

"Don't be so hard on yourself, okay?" Masuo pressed their foreheads together. "If I hadn't been beating the crap out of the cheater, I wouldn't have gone into that elevator. I'm still not sure I could bring myself to do it again. But I did it. Just like you stayed the night by yourself."

Hayato's heart wanted to burst. He squeezed Masuo's hand. "I want to help you get into more elevators."

"I'd like that." Masuo smiled. "But only if I can help you sleep through more nights alone."

"I couldn't ask for anything more."

EPILOGUE

Months later...

It always took some finagling for Masuo and Hayato to match their days off, but since Masuo had finally earned a full-time worker, it had gotten a little easier. Sure, he'd left the guy an hour-by-hour checklist, but he'd stopped calling on things a few months back.

Masuo stepped out of the elevator and stopped in front of Hayato's apartment door. He checked his pockets to make sure he had everything, then knocked.

"We have to be quiet. Kaori finally settled down." Hayato opened the door enough for Masuo to slip inside.

"Look at you being a good uncle."

"I figured Subaru and Fumiko could use a good night's sleep."

Hayato's furniture style ended up being a cozy and eccentric mix of colors and textures, like he'd stumbled upon a basket of a grandma's scrap fabric and told the upholstery shop to use it all. Masuo sat on the blue velvet sofa, the only thing that wasn't seven different colors, while Hayato rested his head on Masuo's lap. A baby monitor lay on the large, tufted-cushion coffee table.

Their conversation flowed as it always did. Hayato played with Masuo's hand while they recounted the events of the past few days.

"I came out to my parents," Masuo said.

Hayato's eyes widened. "How did they take it?"

"Pretty well. I'd been dropping hints about it for the past year, so I'm sure they knew something was coming."

"They're probably holding out hope you'll end up with a woman."

"I don't think so. I told them about you and how wonderful you are."

Hayato rolled his eyes. "They probably hate me now."

"No. They want to meet you."

"That would be one awkward dinner."

"They want to meet the man I want to marry."

Masuo slid off the sofa and got down on one knee. Hayato's mouth dropped open. His rose-colored lips moved, but no words came out. Masuo pulled out the ring, a slim-profile silver ring with amethyst gems.

"When I close my eyes and think about the future, I can't picture it without you by my side," Masuo said. "I know not all of Japan accepts gay marriage yet, but Shibuya has, and I'm sure more cities will fall in line."

"Yes!" The word finally flew from Hayato's lips.

Hayato hugged Masuo, but in his excitement, he ended up falling off the sofa, and they both thumped to the floor. They laughed, and Hayato kissed Masuo. Their first kiss as fiancés, and Masuo knew he would never tire of Hayato's cherry-flavored kisses.

"We'll have to throw a party to celebrate," Hayato said.

"We could invite Subaru and Fumiko."

"And Arashi and Kira."

They had finally started dating a few months back. So far, they were going strong.

Hayato held out his hand. "Put it on me."

Masuo looked around for the ring. "It must've fallen out of my hand."

They both got on their knees and searched for the ring, laughing at how they'd been engaged for less than three minutes and had already lost the ring.

"Found it! It got knocked under the coffee tuft." Hayato gazed down at the ring. "You got me one with amethysts."

Masuo smiled and scooted over to Hayato. "At first, I thought about having a replica of Fumiko's ring made, since you told me that story about your mom wanting it passed down, but then I thought Fumiko has it, and she could give it to Kaori, so I thought we could start our own tradition with this ring."

Hayato rubbed his eyes. "I'd like that."

Masuo slipped the ring onto Hayato's finger and sealed it with a kiss. So far, they'd challenged and sacrificed to make each other better, but Masuo knew their challenges and sacrifices had built a solid foundation for their love to span decades.

THANKS FOR READING!

Most people look at the reviews before reading a new book. Join the crowd and leave a written review where you bought the book to help everyone out.

AUTHOR NOTE

Thanks so much for reading. I wrote most of this story during the summer and fall of the plague year of 2020. It was nice to have that distraction. There is an expression about how artists use their art to exorcise their demons, so many parts of this book helped me work through so much... I'm going to blame the plague for letting all that surface again after so many years. As always, if you're feeling depressed or unwell, please seek help.

Addicted to Lust allowed me to hit the romance button I need to be pressing once a year and mixed well with my love of yakuza fiction. For me, it was the perfect marriage of the two. I hope the first in the Yakuza Path Romance series did the same for you! It is a spinoff my thriller series, the Yakuza Path. The *Romance* allows me to spend more time on the side characters and lets me push the romance button that I usually can't see underneath all the blood that gets spilled in the thrillers.

If Hayato and Subaru sound like familiar names and you've read my Yakuza Path series, then you're right! They made an appearance as side characters in *Flowers of Flesh and Blood* and will continue to be in the thriller series for the foreseeable future. So if you don't mind a lot more blood, check out that book. If you're one of these people who care about timelines, *Addicted to Lust*, excluding the epilogue, takes place before *The Yakuza Path: The Deafening Silence.*

The people subbed to my newsletter got to read this story before anyone else. If you subscribe, then you, too, can read the next Yakuza Path Romance called *My Heart's Desire.* Sign up today at www.amytasukada.com/free-stuff.

ABOUT THE AUTHOR

International best-selling author Amy Tasukada writes thrilling times of crime, love, and gore. Readers who crave diverse characters, unique settings, and edge-of-your-seat action will devour her Yakuza Path series. When Amy isn't writing, she can be found drinking tea in a frilly dress, bending to the will of her cat, and planning her next trip to Japan. Amy identifies as queer and is a sought-after speaker for her lectures on author newsletters, writing LGBT+ characters, and cultural proficiency, diversity, and inclusion.

Connect with Amy on her website
www.amytasukada.com

 facebook.com/amytasukadaofficial
 twitter.com/amytasukada
 youtube.com/amytasukada

CONTACT RESOURCES

FOR CONFERENCES / WRITING WORKSHOPS

Amy is a sought-after speaker available for both online and in-person workshops. Feel free to reach Amy at contact@amytasukada.com so she can teach at your writing conference, club, or group.

Classes Include:

- Making Your Newsletter Work for You
- Building Your Novel and Series Bible
- An Authors' Guide to Wellness
- Writing with Cultural Proficiency, Diversity, and Inclusion in Mind
- Exploring the Rainbow: An LGBTQIA+ 101 for Writing Beyond the Gay Best Friend

FOR READERS

Amy loves to hear from readers! You can email, or send snail mail to:

Amy Tasukada
P.O. Box 111245 | Carrollton, TX 75011

Don't forget to sign up for Amy's newsletter to receive your exclusive monthly chapter of her upcoming release.

FOR BOOK CLUBS

Amy would be happy to speak at your book club via online platform for free. Have five or more people who have already read one of Amy's books ready, and she will Zoom/Skype/FaceTime in for a half hour. It will be tons of fun. To schedule, email contact@amytasukada.com.

FOR LIBRARIANS/BOOKSELLERS

Amy's books are available in the Ingram system and can be ordered for your library or bookstore there.

FOR SUBSIDIARY RIGHTS AGENTS

All Amy's books are available for purchase of subsidiary rights. Please email contact@amytasukada.com if you are interested in harvesting rights.

CPSIA information can be obtained
at www.ICGtesting.com
Printed in the USA
LVHW112056110821
695091LV00004B/159